“Aaron, I don’t want to be *just* friends.”

“You don’t?” Aaron murmured.

Willa shook her head, afraid to speak her heart. Afraid to hear his response. “Do you?”

“I don’t, but—”

She touched her finger to his mouth to silence him. “I don’t care about the *buts*, and...and I don’t think you do either.” She returned her hand to his shoulder. “I want to be yours and you to be mine.”

He exhaled, still holding her. “Willa, we can’t—”

“No one has to know,” Willa interrupted. “We’ll figure something out. I know we will.”

He looked down at her, his face contorted in uncertainty, and Willa rested her head against his chest again. She didn’t care if it was foolish; she didn’t care if there was no way this could end well. She loved him. It was as simple as that.

“Willa.” He breathed her name. “I—”

“Aaron!” came Eleanor’s voice, followed by running footsteps.

Willa was able to pull out of his arms and take a step back before her sister burst into the room.

Emma Miller lives quietly in her old farmhouse in rural Delaware. Fortunate enough to have been born into a family of strong faith, she grew up on a dairy farm, surrounded by loving parents, siblings, grandparents, aunts, uncles and cousins. Emma was educated in local schools and once taught in an Amish schoolhouse. When she's not caring for her large family, reading and writing are her favorite pastimes.

Books by Emma Miller

Love Inspired

Seven Amish Sisters

Her Surprise Christmas Courtship
Falling for the Amish Bad Boy
The Teacher's Christmas Secret
An Unconventional Amish Pair
Her Forbidden Christmas Match

The Amish Spinster's Courtship
The Christmas Courtship
A Summer Amish Courtship
An Amish Holiday Courtship
Courting His Amish Wife
Their Secret Courtship

Visit the Author Profile page at LoveInspired.com for more titles.

Her Forbidden Christmas Match

EMMA MILLER

PLEASE RECYCLE
THIS PRODUCT IS RECYCLABLE
Recycling programs for this product may not exist in your area.

ISBN-13: 978-1-335-93145-0

Her Forbidden Christmas Match

For questions and comments about the quality of this book, please contact us at CustomerService@Harlequin.com.

Love Inspired
22 Adelaide St. West, 41st Floor
Toronto, Ontario M5H 4E3, Canada
www.LoveInspired.com

Printed in Lithuania

He that is soon angry dealeth foolishly.
—*Proverbs* 14:17

Chapter One

Honeycomb, Delaware
Autumn

"Hire a matchmaker?" Willa Koffman turned to her oldest sister, annoyed. "You want *me* to hire a matchmaker?" The idea was ridiculous. Who hired a matchmaker except those who couldn't find a husband on their own? Willa was not that kind of girl.

Willa and Eleanor stood in the kitchen of their family's general store making dough for Christmas cookies. The store sold all sorts of household items for Amish and English customers, but their homemade soups, casseroles and baked goods flew off the shelves faster than they could make them. With the holidays fast approaching, it wasn't too soon to bake cookies to freeze.

"A matchmaker for Willa!" Jane, the youngest of the seven Koffman sisters, entered the kitchen laughing, a basket of fresh eggs in her hand. "That's insulting, Ellie. She's the prettiest girl in Honeycomb. Any boy in the county would walk out with her."

Willa added a scoop of white chocolate chips to the cowboy cookie recipe she was trying. "*Danki*, Jane," she said, appreciating her sister's support.

Eleanor planted a hand on her hip, looking more like their late mother every day. Eleanor was taller than their *dat*, as their *mam* had been, and had a commanding way about her.

"*Ya*, everyone wants to take her home from a singing or for a buggy ride," Eleanor acknowledged. "But do any of them want to marry her? *That's* the question." She turned back to Willa. "I'm sorry. It's not my intention to be unkind, but it's true. You're twenty-four years old, nearly twenty-five. You've dated every eligible man in the county without a single marriage proposal. Not *one*." She held up a finger to emphasize her point.

"I got close with Enoch," Willa reminded, still irritated.

"And you sent him packing." Eleanor pursed her lips. "His aunt told me you broke his heart."

Willa drew back. "We only went out three times. How could I have broken his heart? Enoch is good-looking and nice enough, but I couldn't see spending the rest of my life with him." She dumped a bag of shredded coconut into the mixing bowl. "He sniffed a lot."

Jane set the eggs on the end of the counter near the double ovens and unwound a wool scarf. "I didn't like Enoch. I don't care how many delis his parents own in Lancaster." She slipped out of her coat. "Willa's right. He did sniff all the time. He said he had allergies, but who has—"

"Jane," Eleanor interrupted, setting down the knife she'd been using to cut off portions of sweet yellow butter. "Thank you for bringing more eggs from the henhouse, but Willa and I are trying to talk privately. Would you check the woodstove out front?"

Jane cut her eyes at Willa as if asking if she needed further moral support.

Willa couldn't help but admire the ease with which Jane went up against Eleanor. She tilted her head toward the sales floor where they had the big woodstove. Even though it was nearly November, they'd started their holiday hours and would be opening for the day in a few minutes. "I'm fine. Stoke the fire. It's not expected to get much above freezing for the next few days."

Jane harrumphed and left the room.

Eleanor began cracking eggs into a glass bowl,

tossing the shells into a compost bucket. "I'm serious, Willa," she said softly. "Your method of finding a husband obviously isn't working. You've walked out with plenty of nice boys who could have been good options."

"No one I've dated has been right for me." Willa used a wooden spoon to fold the ingredients in the bowl.

"Because you don't want them to be. You self-sabotage before anyone gets a chance."

That comment made Willa angry. She did no such thing. "What right do *you* have to tell me I need to hurry up and find a husband? You're twenty-eight years old. I don't see you with any offers of marriage." The moment the words came out of her mouth, she regretted them. Even though Eleanor was wrong about why no one would want to marry her, she knew her sister's decision had to be painful even if she wouldn't admit it.

Eleanor flashed her a warning glance. That subject was not one her big sister was willing to discuss. As far as Ellie was concerned, she was already an old maid and always would be. Their eldest sister had it in her head that no one would ever marry her because she'd had her leg amputated below the knee as a child due to a birth defect. But she wore regular shoes. Her prosthetic looked no different from her other leg beneath the skirt of her dress.

"I think it's time we call on Sara Yoder," Eleanor continued. "Mothers from Ohio, Indiana, Wisconsin and all over the United States send their sons and daughters here to find spouses. Sara had more matches than she could count last year, and every one of those couples is now happily married."

Willa added a bag of dark chocolate chunks to her bowl. She was tired of this conversation and of being reminded that her sisters Millie, Beth, Cora and Henry had successfully found husbands. "Who says I even want to get married?" she argued. She did want to marry, and was disappointed that she hadn't found the right man yet, but it galled her that Eleanor was making it sound like it was all her doing. As if something made men want her as a girlfriend on their arms but never saw her as a potential wife. It wasn't her fault that everyone thought she was so pretty. *Gott* had made her this way.

"Not want to get married?" Eleanor scoffed. "Of course you want to get married! Every Amish girl wants to marry."

Except you, Willa thought but didn't say it out loud. There was no telling how badly Eleanor would react. Willa knew Ellie was under a lot of pressure. She had too many responsibilities between running the store, overseeing the care of their father, who had dementia, and trying to help her best friend's now-widowed husband care for his children. However, this morning Willa was struggling to have patience with her sister.

Movement outside the kitchen window caught Willa's eye and she watched a blue car with one red door pull in behind the building. She didn't recognize it. It wasn't a delivery for the store and couldn't be an English customer because they parked in the gravel lot out front. A man with dark hair and a short, scraggly beard was driving.

"It's your duty to be a wife and a mother," Eleanor continued. "Every Amish woman is expected to marry. It's *Gott*'s will that—"

"Who do we know in a blue car with a red door?" Willa interrupted.

"What?"

Willa watched the car lurch to a stop. "Blue car, red passenger door. A man just parked out back like he's supposed to be here."

Eleanor glanced out the window. "Who knows? Maybe Jack's new hire?"

"What new hire?"

Eleanor waved in dismissal. "I thought I told everyone. Jessop Raber asked Jack to hire one of his relatives as a favor. The man's a cousin or maybe a nephew. I can't remember."

Willa's brow creased. "Jessop has Englisher relatives?" Jessop and Sissy Raber owned the local feed store and were pillars of the Amish community.

"I don't know the details. He's just come to Honeycomb after trouble elsewhere and needed a job. Jack offered him one."

Jack was married to their sister Beth. They had recently moved from the apartment above the store into their new house, which could be seen from the store windows. Jack was the contractor who had built the store, so naturally when Eleanor realized they needed more room for their expanding business, their brother-in-law was hired.

"You're avoiding the conversation." Eleanor then launched into how Willa knew very well that she wanted a husband and was just being difficult.

Willa only half listened; when Eleanor got wound up, she could go on for a good half hour without taking a breath. Instead, Willa watched the man through the window as he parked and poured something from a thermos into the plastic lid. He was a big man like her brother-in-law Tobit but with light brown hair. He had a scowl on his face. Movement in the back seat caught her eye. Were there *two* workmen in the car? She frowned. "You think this Raber cousin or nephew is here today to work?" she asked, glancing in her sister's direction. "In this weather?"

Eleanor shrugged. "Jack said something last night about a holdup at one of his other jobs, and with our concrete foundation already cured, he decided to start putting the walls up." She hesitated. "Willa, have you heard anything I've said?"

Willa squinted as she tried to see through the frosty windowpanes from where she was standing at the center island. She was certain now that someone was in the car's back seat. Was it another Englisher needing employment that Jack had taken pity on? He was always hiring someone with a sad story and no money in his pocket. "*Ya*, I'm listening," Willa said absently. "You said Jack is starting on framing up the walls because there's a holdup elsewhere."

"I'm talking about the matchmaker." Eleanor's tone was impatient. "*Schweschter*, you wouldn't have to commit to a match right there and then. We could visit Sara Yoder and see if she might have someone in mind for you. Someone from out of town."

Willa set down her wooden spoon and walked to the window to better see what was going on outside. The man in the car's front seat turned toward the back seat and said something. She rubbed away the condensation on the glass and her jaw dropped. "That man you said Jack hired? I think he has a little girl with him."

Eleanor rolled her eyes. "No one brings a child to an outdoor construction site this time of year. Tell me why you're so opposed to simply *talking* to the matchmaker. Jeb Lapp told me the other day that he's considering hiring Sara to find his Annie a husband."

Willa turned from the window to look at her sister. Annie had been Millie's best friend in their school days. Over the years, Annie had become a good friend to all the Koffman sisters. On a good day, their *dat* called Annie his eighth daughter. On a day when he struggled with his memory, he thought she *was* one of his daughters.

Willa crossed her arms over her chest, upset to hear about Jeb's intention. Annie hadn't said a thing to her about the possibility of an arranged marriage even though they'd spent all Saturday together doing inventory in the store. Annie had started working part-time a few months ago, mostly to get out of a house full of men. "Why does Jeb think Annie needs a matchmaker? Because she's heavy?" She laughed but didn't think it was funny. "That's ridiculous. Millie's fat and look at the man she married. Elden's as handsome as he can be, smart and funny and… And he doesn't care what Millie weighs!" she finished indignantly.

Eleanor scowled and moved her mixing bowl to the stand mixer on the counter. "Don't get yourself all worked up. I think Jeb is concerned about his daughter's prospects, is all. My point is that there's no shame in an arranged marriage. Annie will make a fine wife to a man blessed to have her." She softened her tone. "And your husband will be blessed to have you as his wife, no matter how the match is made."

"I don't want someone else to choose my husband for me," Willa said firmly. "And someone from another state? No way. I'm never leaving Kent County or my family." She turned back to the window, upset by what she was seeing. "He *does* have a little girl with him!"

She could now see clearly through the window and into the car. On the back seat sat a little girl in a pink puffy coat who looked about three or maybe four years old. She wore a knit hat with a big pink pom-pom and had long blond braids. The man handed her a box of crayons and what looked like a stack of coloring books. "He brought a little girl with him," Willa threw over her shoulder. "You don't think Jack's hire intends to leave her in that car while he works?"

Eleanor made a face. "Of course not. He's probably not Jack's new hire. People come and go here all the time." She glanced over her shoulder at a clock on the wall. "Oh dear, it's nearly seven. I have to go. Could you finish mixing this and put the dough in the freezer? A driver is picking me up at the house in half an hour and I need to change into my town clothes."

"I'll take care of it. Where are you going?" Willa didn't take her eye off the girl and the man in the car.

"I told Jon I would take the children to their pediatrician's office so he can go to work." She pulled off her heavy-duty apron and hung it on one of the pegs on the wall. "I'm afraid Emmy and Jamie both have ear infections again."

Willa groaned. "Poor babies." Eleanor's friend Sara had passed away in the spring and she'd been helping the widowed husband, Jon, with their two young children. Eleanor cooked and cleaned for the family, made meals and babysat whenever Sara's mother couldn't.

"Thankfully, neither is too sick." Eleanor sighed. "But Emmy complained yesterday of an earache, and Jon said Jamie was pulling on his ears after I left." She halted in the doorway and sighed again. "I know *Gott* never gives us more than we can bear, but I worry about Jon.

He works so hard and he's a good *dat*, but how's a man supposed to work, cook, clean and care for two small children?"

Willa pressed her lips together. "I pray for them every day."

"As do I." As Eleanor left the kitchen, she said, "I'll be back as soon as I can. Hopefully in time for closing."

"We can close without you. No need to hurry," Willa called after her.

The moment Eleanor was gone, Willa returned to the window. The man and girl were still sitting in the car, talking now. So maybe he wasn't the Raber relative, come to work. But why was the car parked behind the store, then? She crossed her arms, continuing to study them. She considered going outside to ask him what he was doing in their driveway but decided against it. She'd just keep an eye on him.

But if he took *one step* out of that car, leaving that child… he would be sorry.

Aaron Raber sipped black coffee from the cup with the thermos he'd bought at a thrift store over the weekend. He and his daughter had found all kinds of things for themselves and the motel room they were renting. The pay-by-the-week room had a hot plate for cooking and a small refrigerator, but the few pots, pans and dishes there were too nasty for him to risk using. They'd purchased a box of cookware and dishes at the store for ten dollars. He got a handful of mismatched flatware and a kids' metal lunchbox for another four. He also found three pairs of leggings, two sweaters and a flannel shirt for Maggie. She was the one who spotted the pink coat and matching hat on a discount rack. The coat was a good find because she didn't have one; they'd never needed heavy winter clothes in Paraguay. He'd borrowed a few things like a work coat from one of his cousins for fear of running out of money before getting paid. It was hard to believe he'd spent most of the money he'd saved for the last few years just getting to Delaware, but he didn't regret it.

"What color do you think I should make her hair, Papa?" Maggie asked.

He glanced over the seat past her, looking through the back window. Jack Lehman, who had hired him, had said to expect to start work at seven, but it was a few minutes after and there was still no sign of the foreman. According to his new boss, the Mennonite man, Mark, would drive a white truck. No white truck so far.

"Papa." Maggie tugged on the sleeve of his sweatshirt.

He had no sweaters but doubled up on the

two sweatshirts he owned. They would keep him warm enough under his cousin's coat. "Yes, Maggie?" He reached over the seat and tickled her belly. "Did you call for the tickle monster?" he teased.

"No tickle monster!" She giggled, pushing him away.

He laughed and withdrew his hand. "What was the question?"

"What color should her hair be?" She pointed to a page of the coloring book he'd gotten her at the dollar store to keep her busy while he worked.

He'd bought crayons, too, and a sketch pad. And she had books they'd gotten at the library and dollies they'd brought to Delaware with them. Cloth dollies her mama had made for her. Thinking of Ancke made his throat tighten and he looked down at the blank coloring page. Who would have thought that after four years without her, he'd still miss her so much? He forced himself to sound cheerful. "I don't know. What color do you think her hair should be?"

Maggie pursed her lips in deep concentration. "Maybe like mine?" Her face brightened. "Or yours."

He smiled at his daughter, his heart swelling with his love for her. "I think you should give her blond hair." Movement in the store window caught his attention and he looked out. His face fell. A young woman was watching them… Amish. She had to be because she wore a white prayer *kapp*. When their gazes met, she stepped out of view.

Aaron returned his attention to his daughter and tugged playfully on one braid. "Blond hair like yours."

She looked up at him with big nut-brown eyes and solemnly said, "You said Mama had blond hair like me."

He nodded, not trusting himself to speak. They had no photos of his wife; their church hadn't permitted photography. And Ancke had died when Maggie was a baby so she had no memory of her mother. He couldn't decide if that was good or bad. Likely both. "She did." He smiled down at her. "You have her hair and my eyes."

"Brown," Maggie said. She carefully took a yellow crayon from the box on the seat beside her. "I'll give her blond hair like Mama and brown eyes like yours."

"And then she'll look like you," he said.

She nodded, coloring the long locks of hair on the girl on the page. "You want to color with me?"

"Nah, I can't. I have to work, remember?"

"I don't want you to work," she said without

looking up. "Then we could play marbles or color together."

"I know, but Papa has to work, right? We talked about this. You're going to stay in the car and color, play with dollies and look at your picture books, and Papa's going to work."

She shook her head slowly, solemn again. "And I'm not staying with Aunt Sissy because we stick together." She was small for a five-year-old but wise beyond her years.

He imitated her head shake. "You're not staying with Aunt Sissy because we stick together."

"And you're gonna work so we can buy ice cream. Like we had on the *airpane*."

He smiled. She was so smart. Surely no five-year-old was as smart as she was. "Like the airplane," he repeated, saying the word correctly.

Aaron checked his wristwatch again. It was now fifteen after seven. Where was this Mark guy?

Aaron knew nothing about construction but when his uncle Jessop had introduced him to Jack at his feed store, the contractor had insisted that if he were smart and would do as he was told, they'd make him a rough carpenter in no time. Aaron didn't admit he wasn't interested in being a carpenter. But at this point in his life, he'd been thankful to be offered any job far away from his family and the commercial cattle business.

He took another sip of coffee and wondered if the job had been canceled for the day because of the weather. He hoped not. He wasn't excited about working outside in the cold he hadn't known since he was a boy, but he *was* excited about being able to continue to buy food and pay the motel bill.

Maggie started chattering about what kind of ice cream they would buy at the store when he got paid on Friday and he smoothed out the blanket on the car's front seat. He'd brought it in case Maggie got cold. His new boss had explained that one week's pay was usually held back when a man started working for him. However, because of Aaron's circumstances, Jack intended to pay him for the full week this Friday. Aaron didn't know how much his uncle had told Jack about how he ended up in Honeycomb. He tried not to think about it because, since he and Maggie had walked out of the church compound where they lived in the middle of the night, he'd told himself that nothing mattered but getting his little girl to safety. Maggie was his whole world and he was all she had.

Emotion tightened his throat again and he looked up. There was the Amish woman again.

Watching them from the window. He set his jaw in irritation.

He had half a mind to get out of the car and bang on the store's back door. When the woman opened it, he'd ask her why she was spying on him. He'd had enough prying, tattling women back at the compound to last him a lifetime.

The sound of tires on gravel caught Aaron's attention and he spotted a white pickup truck pulling in. The vehicle passed him and the driver waved. There were two Amish men in the truck, too. A crew of four, that's what Jack told him. He'd be working on a crew of four this week to get the exterior walls up for the store's addition.

Aaron dumped the last bit of coffee into his mouth and popped the cup onto the thermos. "Papa has to start work now, but I'll be back shortly to check on you. Remember, I'll never be far away. You can see me right through the windshield." He pointed at the concrete block foundation thirty feet from the car's hood. "But you stay in the car, right?" He looked over the seat. "You do not get out under any circumstances. You need me, you holler. I'll hear you through that window that's cracked open." He pointed to the rear passenger window.

"Right," Maggie echoed, looking up at him with her sweet face. "I stay here. And we're having peanut butter sammies and apples out of my new Nooby Pew lunchbox when it's lunch-time."

He couldn't help but laugh. "Scooby Doo," he corrected gently.

"Scooby Doo," she repeated. "And one of Aunt Sissy's cookies if we're very good," she added enthusiastically.

"And maybe there'll be another visit from the tickle monster," he told her, tickling her belly through her coat again.

The squeal of his daughter's laughter gave him the courage to pull his knit cap over his head and open the car door. "See you soon. I love you, Maggie."

"Love you, Papa," she said without looking up from her coloring book. "Have a good work."

He smiled as he grabbed the borrowed coat and stepped out into the cold morning, closing the door behind him. He took a few steps toward the now-parked truck. There was movement in the extended cab, but no one had yet exited. He figured the guys were getting a last swig of coffee and gathering coats and hats as he had.

A sound from the store caught his attention. A door opening. Then slamming shut. He turned to see a woman in a blue dress, black stockings and leather shoes coming down a short flight of steps as she hastily wrapped a wool shawl around her shoulders.

It was the woman he'd seen in the window.

"What do you think you're doing?" she called, her breath frosty in the morning air.

She had a face like an angel: heart-shaped with rosy cheeks and ripe strawberry lips. Golden-blond wisps of hair fell from her prayer *kapp* to frame her incredible loveliness. She looked like one of those models he'd seen on the covers of magazines in the airport. The only thing that marred her beauty was the scowl on her face.

Aaron was so startled by her words and tone that he glanced over his shoulder, wondering if she was speaking to someone else. Someone she knew. Maybe one of the men in the truck?

"*Ya*, I'm talking to you." She pointed her finger at him. "You can't leave that little girl in a car in this weather. Do you have any idea how irresponsible that is? How dangerous?"

Aaron glanced at the car. Maggie was still busy coloring and hadn't seen her.

He returned his gaze to the Amish woman, immediately disliking her. What right did she think she had to tell him what to do with his daughter? He'd left his community to escape from other people telling him what to do with his daughter and how to raise her. This woman didn't even know him. Somehow that made her criticism doubly inappropriate, but he'd known women like her before—too pretty for their own good. Somehow thinking that made them entitled.

He glanced back at the truck; the foreman was getting out. He needed to introduce himself. The sooner the day started, the sooner it would end, and he and Maggie could go home to their shabby motel room and play marbles. He looked back to the Amish woman as she approached and lowered his voice so his new boss wouldn't hear. "Mind your own business, lady," he murmured.

Instead of backing away, she took another step toward him. "A little girl alone in the cold *is* my business," she told him, her big brown eyes flaring angrily.

Her speech and manner were bold and that surprised him. In their community in Paraguay, women were soft-spoken and docile. No woman ever confronted a man this way. According to their bishop's preaching, it wasn't how God intended the world to be. Her tone knocked him so off-kilter that it took him a moment to respond. "I… She's fine. She's warm in her coat and hat and there's a blanket if she needs it. I'm here to work." He motioned toward the addition.

"Her mother can't watch her?"

He looked directly into her eyes. "Again, not your business, but she doesn't have one," he answered stoically. He was surprised when she softened her tone as she spoke again. Her face gentled, making her all the prettier. That annoyed him even more.

"You're the Rabers' cousin, right?" she asked, pulling her shawl closer. It was windy and bitter outside.

"I'm Jeb's nephew. Aaron." He looked over his shoulder. The driver was unloading tools from the bed of the truck. "Look, I have to get to work," he told the busybody.

She glanced into the car, then back at him. "What's your daughter's name?"

He exhaled impatiently. "Maggie."

"I'm Willa, Willa Koffman. I live back there." She pointed at a white farmhouse in the distance down a long lane. A large barn, outbuildings and a windmill dotted the surrounding barnyard. "My sisters and father and I own the store." She looked at his daughter again. "Do you think Maggie would like to come inside and make Christmas cookies with me and my sisters?"

After all they'd been through, the thought of having Maggie out of his sight sent a wave of panic through Aaron. He'd come so close to losing his daughter that he wasn't sure he'd ever be able to again. He met the woman's gaze.

"So that she can stay warm. And have some fun," she added.

He ground out his words one syllable at a time. "Ab-so-lute-ly not." Thinking that was the end of their conversation, he walked away from her.

But she followed right in his footsteps. "Hey! I'm not done with you, Aaron!"

Chapter Two

"Don't you walk away from me!" Setting her jaw, Willa followed the big man. When he didn't turn around, she tapped him on the shoulder. "I'm still talking to you!"

"Good morning. Aaron, right?" Willa heard Mark Miller call from his truck. He was one of Jack's foremen and must have just arrived to start work on the addition.

Aaron raised his hand awkwardly, greeting Mark while ignoring Willa. "That's me."

"He'll be there in a minute, Mark!" Willa called, shivering in the cold.

Aaron whipped around to face her. "I have to go." He spoke quietly but his voice strained with irritation. "It's my first day. And I need this job."

"Then you best get to work." She crossed her arms. "If Maggie's inside with me, you won't have to worry about her." She flashed a fake smile not knowing why this stranger had so quickly gotten under her skin. "That way, you'll be able to concentrate on your work. And your daughter won't be cold and lonely."

He looked down at her, his face hard. "I have to go," he repeated.

"I understand. But a girl so young needs a sitter. I'm surprised Sissy Raber didn't offer—you being relatives."

He glanced down at his work boots, which needed replacing.

"She did offer, but...but Maggie doesn't like being apart from me." He met her gaze. "It's just the two of us." His eyes were dark brown with little lines of gold in them.

Willa felt her heart soften as she heard the emotion in his voice. She was annoyed with this man for being irresponsible with his child, but something in his tone gave her pause. He loved the little girl; she could see it in his eyes. She could also see that he was torn about what to do.

She glanced over her shoulder. The girl watched them now, her nose pressed to the window. Willa hesitated a moment, then walked over to the car.

"Hey!" Aaron called after her.

Willa smiled at his daughter peering at her through the window. "Hi, I'm Willa," she said. "Your dad says your name's Maggie."

Maggie drew back from the window, looking frightened.

Willa kept smiling. Of course the child was shy; all children were cautious with strangers. "Maggie? Is that right? Or was he telling me a fib?" she teased softly, hoping to put her at ease.

The girl slid closer to the window, then spoke through the crack. "I'm Maggie Mae Raber," she whispered.

"And who's that? Someone you know?"

The little girl nodded, her brown eyes wide. "That's my papa. He has a job."

Willa heard Aaron come up behind her but ignored him. It was so cold out that her nose was beginning to feel numb and she wished she hadn't come outside without her heavy wool cloak. "That's what he told me. Are you going to watch him work today?"

Maggie hesitated, still unsure if she should be talking to Willa, but then she held up a coloring book. "I'm going to color."

Willa could tell now that Maggie was older than she'd first thought. The girl sounded more mature and spoke better than a three-or four-year-old. She was simply tiny. "That sounds like fun. Guess what I'm doing today?"

Maggie's breath frosted the window, her curiosity stronger than her fear. "What?"

Willa opened her eyes wide. "Making cookies!"

Maggie's jaw dropped. She wiped the condensation on the glass. “I never made cookies before. Papa buys them in a bag at the dollar store.”

Willa leaned closer. “Never made cookies?” she exclaimed, glancing over her shoulder at the hulking man behind her who was so close that he blocked the bitter wind. She returned her attention to Maggie. “I think we should remedy that. I could ask your papa if you could help me today. Would you like that?”

Again, Maggie hesitated, then murmured, “I would love that!”

“Aw, that’s playing dirty,” Aaron muttered quietly enough for only Willa to hear.

“We could even bake cookies for you to take home so your papa doesn’t have to buy them at the store,” Willa continued, feeling mischievous. Maybe this was playing dirty but for a good reason.

“Papa would like that,” Maggie told her.

“Well, let me ask if it’s okay.” Willa turned around to Aaron, nearly bumping into him. “Would it be all right?” she asked quietly. “If Maggie goes inside with me? I won’t take her out of the store, I promise you. And I’ll leave the back kitchen door unlocked. You can walk in anytime to check on her. And you’ll be able to see her through the window.” She pointed to the one she’d watched him from.

He groaned so deep in his throat that it sounded like a growl.

She gazed up at him, wondering if he thought a little growl would discourage her. If he did, he was wrong. "Come on, Aaron. Let her come inside with me. It's perfectly safe. Ask Mark if you want." She gestured in the direction of the white pickup. "He'll vouch for me. For our whole family. His sister Rosie is friends with my sister Beth. And I know your aunt and uncle well," she added, unsure why this was suddenly so important to her. In all fairness, it wasn't unsafe for Maggie to sit in the car with her father working so close. She just hated to see the child cooped up in a cold car all day.

Aaron pressed the heel of his hand to his forehead. She could tell he was considering her proposal.

"And…and you can come inside and have lunch with Maggie," Willa added, hoping to sweeten the pot. "We're having homemade chicken noodle soup and egg salad sandwiches. I made the noodles myself." She had no idea why she said that. What did she care if he knew she could make noodles? "And cookies." She looked up at him. He was a full head taller than she was and broad-shouldered with heavy eyebrows and a square jaw. He might have been attractive without the perpetual scowl on his face.

In a scruffy Englisher-bear kind of way. "You can't say no to cookies your daughter wants to make for you, can you?"

He glowered and looked past Willa to Maggie. "Do you want to go inside with Willa and make cookies while Papa works?"

His daughter met his gaze, hesitated, then sat back on the seat, suddenly tamping her enthusiasm. "I can stay here. I can watch you work," she said in a small, consoling voice.

Her tone and the idea that she was obviously worried about her father made a lump rise in Willa's throat. These two had a very special father/daughter relationship. She could see that.

Aaron opened the car door. "What do you want to do, cupcake?" he asked Maggie. He crouched to be eye to eye with her. "Do you want to make cookies with Willa?"

Maggie gazed up at him and nodded slowly.

Willa saw Aaron smile. It was obvious that he loved her deeply. Adored her.

"All right, then. Fine." He gestured for her to get out of the car. "Go on with you. Papa really does have to get to work." He pointed his finger at her. "Behave yourself. Be helpful, don't make a mess. Mind your manners and do what Willa says."

"Yes, Papa."

Willa held out her hand to the little girl. She

didn't know what had occurred before the two of them arrived in Honeycomb, but seeing how they were with each other, she suspected it had been complicated. And hard. Her heart went out to them both. "And Papa can come and have lunch with you," he said, touching the tip of her button nose with his finger.

Maggie giggled.

Then Willa led her toward the kitchen door and as she passed Aaron, he surprised her by mouthing the words, "Thank you."

"You're welcome," she answered, then hurried the little girl into the warm and cozy kitchen.

At four o'clock, Aaron walked into the shabby pay-by-the-week motel room they were staying in. He was dead tired from the day's cold and physical labor. He didn't mind hard work; he was used to it. He'd worked for his father on the family cattle ranch in Paraguay, six days a week, ten to twelve hours a day, since he was fourteen. But it had been two weeks since he'd done anything so taxing and his muscles ached.

Maggie trotted into the room behind him, chattering a mile a minute. She hadn't stopped talking since he'd retrieved her from the Koffman General Store half an hour ago.

"And—and I got to pour in the chocolate

chips," his daughter gushed. "Two kinds! Dark chocolate and milk chocolate. Willa said that makes the cookies better." She set a big white plastic tub full of cookies on the tiny table near the door where they ate. Aaron had tried to refuse them, but Willa wouldn't take no for an answer and two sisters had backed her up.

"And Willa says you brown the butter." Maggie slipped off her backpack that contained her dollies and books and left it by the door. "Willa says you never brown butter for sugar cookies." She pursed her lips. "Unless they're her *grossmama*'s brown butter sugar cookies and then you do. *Grossmama* means grandmother if you're Amish."

He smiled with amusement; Maggie wasn't yet privy to her father's past. "I happen to know that."

"Willa says—"

"Willa says, Willa says," he interrupted. "Does the woman rise and set in the sky?"

Maggie made a face. "I don't think she can float, Papa. People don't float except on a raft like in my book."

Aaron set down the grocery bag of food containers he'd also tried to refuse and had come home with anyway. It turned out Willa Koffman was more stubborn than he was, at least today. Inside was a jar of the most delicious chicken noodle soup he'd ever had, one of fresh applesauce and a bag of homemade buttermilk biscuits. "I'm guessing you had a good day with Willa." He shrugged off his borrowed coat and dropped it over a chair.

Maggie unzipped hers and put it on top of his. Next, she plucked her pom-pom hat from her head and stuffed it into the coat sleeve the way he'd taught her so she wouldn't lose it. "So much, Papa. And with Jane, too. She's the little sister." She shook her head, her forehead creasing with seriousness. "Not little like me. Big. But Willa says she'll always be her little sister. And Millie is a sister, but not the biggest one. Millie and Willa are twins!"

"Are they?"

"And Millie just had two babies. A boy baby and a girl baby."

"Did she, now?" He dropped onto the twin bed he slept in and removed his boots. He would have to buy a pair of wool socks come payday. The cotton athletic ones he had weren't warm enough. He feared he might have gotten frostbite if it hadn't been for the kitchen's warmth during his lunch break. He'd forgotten how cold winter could be in this part of the world.

Maggie went on talking about this cookie dough and that one she'd made with the Koffman sisters as he rolled off his socks and massaged his feet. He was pleased she'd had such a nice day. As much as he hated to admit it, Willa had been right. Having Maggie inside a warm building doing something fun was a much better plan than keeping her in the car all day. He was thankful for Willa's kindness but didn't like accepting her help. Or anyone else's. It made him feel like he wasn't doing the right thing for his daughter. It made him worry that maybe his parents had been right. Maybe a motherless child shouldn't be raised by a widowed father.

Feeling anger bubble inside him, he balled up the socks and tossed them into the plastic laundry basket near the bathroom door. *They're wrong*, he told himself. *I can do this. I can raise her. I can be a father and a mother to Maggie. I have to be because that's what Ancke wanted.*

"Willa says we can't make cookies or cookie dough to freeze tomorrow," Maggie continued as she carefully removed the biscuits from the paper bag. "We're going to make bread and freeze it. She says we're going to make banana bread and pumpkin bread."

"Oh, you are, are you?" he asked, only half listening.

Maggie froze. "But only if you want me to," she said slowly. She nibbled on her lower lip. "I can sit in the car and watch you do your work, Papa. If you want me to."

His chest tightened with love for her and he smiled. "It sounds to me like Willa needs your help. All that deliciousness to make. I can't keep you from that."

Maggie leaped in the air, clapping her hands together. "Yay! Thank you, Papa."

"You're welcome, cookie," he returned, fighting the urge to lie back and take a little nap before he warmed the soup for supper. He couldn't believe how tired he was, but it was a good tired. For the first time since they escaped, he felt like maybe, *just maybe* he had done the right thing in leaving Paraguay. Not that it had been easy. Good or bad, that life was the only life he had known for the last fifteen years. Those were the only people he knew. Even his aunt and uncle here were strangers; he hadn't seen them in sixteen years.

But the strangers, related and unrelated in Honeycomb, had been kind to him since his arrival. And welcoming and helpful. Jack Lehman hadn't hesitated to offer him a job despite his lack of building experience, and the crew he'd worked with today had been nice to him.

And then there was Willa Koffman.

He'd been so annoyed with her this morning with her interference. But she'd been right about Maggie being better off inside the store with her. As he thought about her pretty face and how she'd pushed her way into their life, he suspected she could be trouble.

What kind of trouble, he couldn't yet say.

That evening, Willa shared a quiet supper of leftovers and fresh buttermilk biscuits with Jane and their father. She had gotten used to having fewer people at the table now that Millie, Cora, Beth and Henry had married, but sitting down with only the three of them had felt odd. Eleanor had still been at Jon Coblenz's caring for his children.

As Willa and Jane finished the dishes, Eleanor rushed in, flustered and looking exhausted. "I'm sorry, I'm sorry," she said, removing her black bonnet and cloak. "I meant to be here in time for supper. Where's *Dat*?" She looked around. "Is he all right? I know he gets worried if I'm out after dark."

"He's fine," Willa assured her as she took the hat and cloak from her sister and hung them in the mudroom. "He ate his supper," she continued, walking back into the kitchen. "Now he's in the parlor with his dominoes." Despite the progression of his dementia, it was a game he could still play and when there was no one around to join him, he amused himself by matching up the tiles over and over again.

"Sit," Willa directed. She turned up the flame

under a pot of stewed chicken and slippery dumplings. She did the same for the small pan of pole lima beans they picked months ago from their garden and froze for the winter. "We saved supper for you. And don't tell us that you ate with the children."

"Because we know better," Jane added.

"No need to go to such fuss." Eleanor waved her hand. "Just a cup of coffee will be enough."

"Who's fussing?" Willa asked, glad she could do something for her big sister. She felt guilty about her reaction to Eleanor's suggestion to hire a matchmaker that morning. She didn't agree with her, but she knew Ellie's heart was in the right place. It always was. Since their mother's death more than three years ago, Eleanor had been the knitting needle that kept their family woven together, even as their sisters married and moved out of the house. "How many times have you saved something for one of us when we got in later than expected?" she continued. "And not usually for reasons as good as yours."

"*Ya*, how often has Willa been late because she was out in a buggy with a beau?" Jane teased.

Willa cut her eyes in warning at the baby of the family, who was no longer a child, but a young woman. She didn't want to discuss her failure at finding a husband, not twice in one day.

"But it's true," Jane argued as she poured Eleanor a cup of coffee from the percolator on the stove. She carried it to the table. "Here you go. Strong and black the way you like."

Eleanor sighed and sat back in her chair, looking as if it was the first time she'd been able to relax all day. "Bless you. *Danki*."

"How are the children?" Willa asked over her shoulder. She opened the still-warm oven and removed a baking sheet with two honey biscuits. "Not too sick, I hope. Did they have ear infections?"

"*Ya*. Jamie in both ears, Emmy in just the one." Eleanor blew out a breath. "It turned out to be a long day, in any case. We had to wait forever to see the pediatrician and then there was more waiting on the prescriptions at the pharmacy. The children were well-behaved, but poor Jon had to stay late at the store and wait on some important customer."

The widower built furniture and sold it in his cousin's store. Mostly he worked at home in his woodshop. But occasionally he had to work in the store showroom; all the men who sold furniture there took turns and Jon refused to let others cover his shift.

Eleanor shook her head. "I'm so glad Jon insisted I get a cell phone after Sara passed."

"Even if Judy said The Bishop wasn't going to like it," Jane put in. Judy was their mother's older sister and her husband was the bishop of their church district. His name was Cyrus, but everyone called him The Bishop, including their aunt.

"With me having a cell phone, Jon's able to get a hold of me when he needs to," Eleanor continued. "He called me to let me know when he was leaving the furniture shop. By the time he got home tonight, the children were fed, bathed and ready for bed, the first dose of antibiotics in them."

"I don't know what Jon would do without you," Willa said, ladling the chicken and dumplings into a bowl. She passed it to Jane to carry to the table.

"We were discussing the fundraiser to help Jon with the rest of Sara's bills." Jane set the bowl on the table. The family had decided to help the Coblenz family financially by holding a Christmas crafts sale at the store; all the proceeds would go to them. Because the Amish didn't believe in insurance, the medical bills still weighed heavily on Jon. "I wondered if we should sell take-out meals, too." She made a face. "Willa thought that was a dumb idea."

"I never said that," Willa corrected. "What I said was that it might be more work than we can handle. I'm not sure we can manage take-out meals without more volunteers than we have now."

Eleanor reached for the spoon already set out for her on a cloth napkin. "Hmm, selling take-out meals." She looked up at them. "I like the idea. We'd make more money. Soups, stews and bread are easy enough to make."

"And we could ask for volunteers at church on Sunday. We don't have to do all the work ourselves," Jane suggested.

"Jane has a point," Willa said, thinking aloud. "Everyone in Honeycomb has been asking what they could do to help Jon and the children. This would be the perfect opportunity. What better gift to give during the Christmas season?"

"Why don't we sleep on the idea," Eleanor suggested. "I'll talk to Beth and Millie about it tomorrow and we'll make our final decision tomorrow over supper." She sampled the chicken and dumplings and added pepper. "How were your days today?"

"Dull," Jane declared, bringing a bowl of the lima beans simmered in chicken broth and butter to Eleanor. She dropped into a chair near her and lowered her chin to her hand. "No one interesting came in."

Eleanor smiled. "You mean no handsome young men?"

"No one anywhere near my age," Jane grumped.

She sat up suddenly. "Oh! But there was a nice-looking man. That guy that Jack hired, Jessop Raber's nephew. I think he likes Willa."

Willa had returned to the stove but whipped around in annoyance. "What? He does not *like* me."

Jane ignored Willa, her eyes widening as she went on talking to Eleanor. "His name's Aaron Raber and he's widowed. With a little girl."

"And he's an *Englisher*," Willa reminded, grabbing a dish towel.

"But I wonder if he *used* to be Amish," Jane returned. She looked at Eleanor. "He's related to the Rabers and he's settling in Honeycomb. Why's he settling here?" She shrugged. "Maybe he wants to be Amish again."

Willa rolled her eyes. "I don't think he used to be Amish, Jane. How would you know anything about him? He didn't say three words to you all day." She walked toward the table.

"Maggie told me," Jane replied.

"That he was Amish."

"Nay," Jane said with a huff. "But Maggie said other things that made me think he might have been."

Eleanor looked from Willa to Jane and back to Willa again. "Wait. Go back. Who is Maggie?"

Willa started to answer but Jane beat her to it. "Aaron's little girl," she said in a rush.

"They lived in Paraguay in South America and just moved here. Maggie told me they live in a motel. Just the two of them. Her *mam* died. I didn't know you could live in a motel."

Eleanor looked at Willa. "She tell you anything else?"

Willa shook her head no.

"*Ach.* The little girl has no mother?" Eleanor asked. "You're talking about the child you saw in that car this morning, *ya*?"

Willa hesitated. She didn't want to talk about Aaron Raber. She'd had a lovely day with Maggie, baking and tidying the store shelves. But when Aaron fetched Maggie at four thirty, he hadn't been a bit friendlier than he had that morning. He'd thanked her for inviting Maggie to spend the day with her but had been noncommittal about whether she could return to the store the following day. And she'd had to practically force him to take cookies his daughter had made. "*Ya*, Maggie is Aaron's daughter," she told her sister.

Eleanor took a bite of a biscuit, nodding thoughtfully. "And why was Jessop's nephew in Paraguay?"

Jane pressed her hands to the table and leaned closer. "That's what I want to know. I was thinking about paying Sissy Raber a visit tomorrow. She'll have details."

"Details that aren't your business. You'll do no such thing," Willa told Jane in a firm voice.

"That poor little girl. Poor man, widowed like Jon. With a child," Eleanor mused. She looked up at Willa. "I hope we're doing everything we can for them. I know kindnesses should be shared year-round, but I can't imagine what it must be like for them to be in a strange town, not knowing many folks this time of year."

Willa folded her arms over her chest. Eleanor was right, of course. She should feel compassion for Aaron instead of this irritation that bordered on anger. She exhaled, trying to release the negative feelings. "I told Aaron that Maggie was welcome to stay with me—with us—during the day."

"What?" Eleanor asked, not seeming pleased. "That's a big commitment. The addition is going to take three months to build." She narrowed her gaze. "This isn't one of your impulsive decisions you're going to regret later, is it?"

"Nay," Willa returned, choosing not to be upset by her sister's comment. It was true that in her younger years, she *had* occasionally made rash decisions, but she wasn't that person anymore. "I can't let her sit in that car all day, can I? So Maggie will stay with us during the day while he's working." She raised her shoulders and let them fall. "At least I hope she is. I'm not

sure he'll let her. He seems like a proud man. It's obvious he doesn't want anything from anyone."

"But Willa made him take leftovers home," Jane said. "And a bunch of cookies."

Eleanor looked at Jane. "Maybe you should pay Sissy a visit tomorrow. Let's put Annie at the register in the morning and that will give you time to go. See what you can find out without seeming too nosy. Take her some of the pumpkin bread we made Saturday." She turned to Willa. "And tomorrow you need to let Aaron Raber know that Maggie is not only welcome, but you want to have her spend time with you because..." She met Willa's gaze thoughtfully. "I have this feeling that *Gott* has brought them to us for a reason. We've been so blessed with how well the store is doing. We can certainly help a family in need. You should find out what we can do for them."

"He's not a man that takes help easily," Willa said.

Eleanor nodded. "You don't have to come right out and ask. Be friendly. Get to know him a bit. He might open up to you."

Willa dropped her hands to her sides. "I agree, we should help folks who need it, but why do I have to be the one to talk to him? I thought you wanted me to concentrate on finding a husband and getting out of your house." The moment the words were out of her mouth, she regretted them. She didn't know what had made her say such a thing. Maybe the conversation she'd had with Eleanor had worried her more than she realized. What was wrong with her that no one wanted to marry her?

Eleanor met her gaze.

"I'm sorry, Ellie," Willa murmured. "That wasn't nice. I know you said what you said this morning because you're concerned."

Eleanor reached out and took Willa's hand, squeezing it before she let go. "I said those things because I want you to be happy. I want you to live a fulfilled life."

"I know." Willa took a deep breath and exhaled. "So we have a plan. You and Jane see what you can find out from Sissy, and I don't know when I'll have the opportunity, but I'll try to talk to Aaron." She threw up her hands. "And we'll leave the rest to *Gott*."

Chapter Three

Thursday morning Aaron pulled his car in behind the Koffman store, his mood as black as the clouds hanging in the dismal sky. The sun had barely risen before the storm had rolled in and now fat, icy raindrops pelted the windshield. Mark wasn't there in his white truck.

"Nooo, Papa. I don't want it to rain," Maggie fussed from the back seat.

It wasn't like her to whine but she had her heart set on spending the day with the Koffman sisters. With Willa, in particular. Before they prayed together the previous night, she'd told him she'd had the best day of her life with Willa.

That had hurt his heart.

Her statement reminded him that not only had *he* suffered emotionally in the South American enclave they had lived in, but that she had, as well. It also stung that her best day had been with Willa and not him. Shouldn't her best days be with her father? He had to struggle not to be bitter about that. Or chastise himself for not being a better father. He was trying to make a new life for them and acknowledged that he had to stay on course and not be sidelined with regrets. As his *grossmama* used to say, "A bucket of regret never makes a spoon of difference."

Sighing, he shifted the car into Park and turned off the wipers. They needed new blades so they weren't doing much to clean the windshield anyway. He left the engine running to keep them warm.

"Papa doesn't want it to rain, either," he said, thinking *no work, no pay.* He was counting on a paycheck for a full forty hours tomorrow and if he didn't get it, there would be things they would have to go without for another week. Even with Willa supplementing their meals heavily by feeding them lunch daily and sending home leftovers for supper, he'd have to cut his budget. He couldn't buy new wiper blades or winter socks for him and Maggie. And he'd have to cancel the Saturday appointment for the car even though it was sorely in need of an oil change and he was worried about a knocking sound in the engine.

"I have to stay, Papa! Willa and me, we're going to make Christmas tree *ormanents* today,"

Maggie said from the back. "From salt dough. And we're gonna paint them!"

He heard the click of her seat belt and she leaned on his seat to peer up at him. "She says Englishers put real trees in the houses for Christmas and hang *ormanents*." She frowned thoughtfully. "She was pulling my leg, Papa. People don't put trees in houses."

"Actually, Englishers do hang *ornaments* on live trees in their homes," he said, pronouncing the word correctly.

Her little blond eyebrows knitted. "For Jesus being born?"

He smiled and tugged on one long braid, impressed with his handiwork. He'd never braided her hair before they left Paraguay, but he'd watched his mother do it for his daughter more times than he could count. "Something like that." He stared out the windshield, watching the rain stream down the glass.

The raindrops reminded him of tears and a lump rose in his throat. He missed his family and his friends. He missed the certainty of a meal and roof over their heads. And he was lonely. The guys in the crew were nice enough, especially Mark, but he hesitated to participate in their conversations. Back in Paraguay, folks were always listening and reporting back to their church leader. There were consequences for stepping out of line in deed or thought. Even knowing it wasn't like that here in Honeycomb, old habits didn't die easily.

Maggie remained where she was and rested her chin on her hands. "Maybe the rain's gonna stop and then you can work and I can make or-na-ments," she said, hope in her voice.

He shook his head. "I don't think it's going to stop. At least not according to the weather forecast."

She dropped back in her seat. "Can I still make ornaments with Willa?" she asked hesitantly.

"Maybe another time." He wondered what they would do all day in the tiny, sad motel room. They could only play Go Fish for so long.

"But, Papa, I want—" Halting midsentence, she excitedly bounced up off the seat. "Papa! Papa, it's Willa!" She pointed. "Willa's waving at me!"

He glanced up and saw her in the kitchen window. She wasn't waving at Maggie; she was beckoning her.

He groaned. So far, he'd managed to avoid Willa while still allowing Maggie to stay with her. Several times over the last two days she had tried to talk with him, asking questions, but he'd dodged any conversation. He'd learned from his aunt Sissy that her sister Jane had visited the Raber farm, peppering Sissy with questions about him and Maggie. He assumed Willa had sent her. However, his aunt had stayed true to her promise and hadn't shared any details of their life before arriving in Honeycomb. He didn't know why he didn't want folks to know about his past. Maybe because he was embarrassed that it had taken him so long after Ancke died to leave that place. Or maybe he didn't want people to judge him. Or maybe he just wanted to put that all behind him. It was likely a combination of all three.

His gaze went to the window again. Now Willa was motioning *him*.

Aaron's impulse was to look away, to pretend he didn't see her. He could declare the day a waste of gasoline, back out and return to the motel. But he didn't look away. For some reason he couldn't…

"She's still waving, Papa. You think she wants us to come inside?" Maggie looked at him, her big brown eyes expectant. "I think she does. We better go in. She has hot chocolate for me in the morning. I think I better get my hot chocolate. But I could share with you."

He groaned.

Maggie waited.

"Fine," he muttered. "We'll go in. But we're not

staying," he warned. "One cup of hot chocolate and then we're returning to the motel."

But Maggie wasn't listening. She was already out the door and running through the rain in her pink coat. She gave him no other choice but to follow her.

Willa opened the back door to see Maggie climb out of the car, slam the door shut and run for the house. She couldn't help but smile as she opened a big black umbrella and hurried down the steps to meet her.

"Willa!" Maggie cried. "Can we make *orma... ornnaments*?"

"That's the plan," Willa answered, watching Aaron close his car door.

Maggie tugged on Willa's apron. "Can we do it fast? Papa says we have to go to the motel 'cause it's raining but I don't like it there." She wrinkled her freckled nose. "I like it here."

Willa watched Aaron trudge slowly toward them. His broad shoulders were hunched, his face sober; he looked like he was attending a funeral. Not that she should be surprised. She didn't think she'd seen him smile since she met him.

Willa hesitated. She had half a mind to take Maggie inside, shut the door and lock it. He could sit in the car and wait for his daughter all day for all she cared. Then, remembering her promise to Eleanor, she pressed her lips together. Her sister had been bugging her for two days to get more information on Aaron's situation. So far she'd learned nothing. At the evening meal tonight, she didn't want to have to admit she still knew nothing. Eleanor was already in a bad mood. They had two deliveries the previous night just as they were closing. Boxes now filled the storage room and spilled into the hall. They had to be inventoried and put in some semblance of order and Ellie had a million other things to do.

Willa lifted the umbrella, pulling Maggie closer to her so she wouldn't get wet. "Looks like there'll be no work today," she called to Aaron. "Want a cup of coffee? Jane made cinnamon rolls. I have to warn you, though." She tried to sound cheery. "She added something called cardamom to them. I hope you like cardamom. Whatever it is."

He scowled but continued toward her. Not sure whether to wait, she ushered Maggie inside and left the door open a crack. "Stand here until we get that wet coat off you," she told the little girl, carefully closing the umbrella so it didn't throw water all over the hardwood floor.

Maggie pulled off her wet knit cap, handed

it to Willa and began to work at the zipper of her coat.

Willa helped her out of her coat.

Maggie stomped her feet on the floor mat and water flew from her soggy canvas sneakers.

"No rain boots?" Willa asked.

Maggie shook her head. Then spotting Jane in the kitchen, she took off, her sneakers squeaking on the floorboards. "Can I have hot cocoa?" she pleaded, her voice bright. "With marshmallows?"

"Already have the kettle on," Jane called.

When the back door swung open, Willa was hanging Maggie's coat and cap on hooks near the door. It had taken Aaron so long to cross the ten feet between the car and the store that she'd wondered if he'd changed his mind about coming in.

His frame filled the doorway and Willa took a step back. The hall was crowded with the two of them and the towers of boxes. She suddenly felt shy, which made no sense because she was not a shy woman. Certainly not around men. Men of all ages liked her, from teens to those in their nineties. They were drawn to her like bees to honey. Folks said it was due to her pretty face, but secretly she hoped it was more than that.

For a moment he stood there, dripping on the

floor, not saying a word. He just looked at her. Which made her nervous.

"Raining hard out there, isn't it?" she remarked with a laugh that echoed strangely off the walls. She didn't sound like herself.

"I'd say so." He looked over his shoulder into the pouring rain. "No work today, I guess. Mark said as much last night, but I was—"

She waited for him to finish what he was saying, but when he didn't, she took another step back and waved him in. It occurred to her that maybe the sour look on his face was disappointment. He was disappointed he couldn't work. An admirable trait in her family. "Close the door before it's as wet inside as out." She pointed at the strip of pegs on the wall. "You know where the coats go." She knew he did because he'd had lunch inside with Maggie the last three days. "Come into the kitchen and have some coffee." She left him there and strode away, vexed with herself for feeling awkward. This place was hers; it was where she felt most comfortable. It was her own fault if she let him get to her.

The kitchen was bustling, as always, for which she was thankful. With all the confusion, maybe she wouldn't feel so uncomfortable in Aaron's presence. Maggie was busy washing her hands at the sink, chattering with Jane. Jane had opened one of their two full-sized ovens to remove the sheet pans of four dozen cinnamon rolls she'd baked. If Willa had any doubts as to how good the new recipe would be, they were gone. The warm scent of cinnamon mixed with the bright-smelling cardamom was even more delightful than the old recipe.

"Do you have enough dough to make another two dozen rolls?" Eleanor called to Jane. She stood on the far side of the room, holding the telephone receiver to her chest so the caller couldn't hear them. "Someone died this morning from Mark and Rosie's church and Rosie wants to take them over to the family this morning."

"I'm sorry to hear that," Henrietta, whom they called Henry, said from the sink where she'd stepped aside to give Maggie room to wash. Henry lived in Rose Valley with her new husband but had made the trip in her buggy despite the rain.

"More dough in the fridge," Jane answered, setting a pan of rolls on a cooling rack on the counter. She went back to the oven for another. "She can have some of these and I'll bake more. Tell her an hour. I can't frost them until they cool."

Eleanor repeated what their sister said into

the phone, nodded and said, “See you then,” before hanging up.

“I can make more coffee,” Henry called as she dried her hands on a dish towel. “Anyone want another cup?”

Willa glanced over her shoulder to see Aaron standing in the doorway watching them. He had that look on his face that she’d seen on other men when they didn’t feel comfortable in a room full of women. “See. You’re just in time for fresh coffee and cinnamon rolls.” Without waiting for him to reply, she turned her back to him. “Aaron wants coffee. And two rolls when you plate them, Jane.”

“I… I don’t need coffee, or—we already ate breakfast,” he sputtered.

“Nonsense,” Eleanor said, walking past him. “Pull up a chair or stool, whatever suits you.” She pointed to the large two-level center island that served as a workspace and a place to eat meals. “You have a darling daughter,” she continued as she returned to the stack of inventory sheets she’d been trying to sort before she answered the phone.

“It’s… It’s kind of you to let her stay with you while I work,” Aaron said, not seeming to know what to do with his hands. Finally, he shoved them into his front pockets. He wore blue jeans and a sweatshirt over a plaid flannel shirt. He wasn't a slender man, but he wasn't fat, either. He looked muscular.

"We enjoy having her, don't we, Willa?" Eleanor asked without looking up from the paperwork on the counter.

"We do." Willa handed Maggie a hand towel when she hopped down from a stool at the sink. "Especially on a rainy day." She crouched so she was eye to eye with the girl. "Because a lot of folks won't come out in this weather to shop so we'll have even more time to make our salt dough ornaments, won't we?" She touched the tip of her button nose with a finger. "But first I think we better have a cinnamon roll and hot chocolate."

Maggie nodded enthusiastically as she dried her hands and looked at her father. "Can I stay, Papa? Please?"

He glanced out the window. "No work for me today. We should probably go."

"There may not be work outside, but plenty here to be done," Eleanor muttered, shuffling pages. "I can't make heads nor tails of this inventory." She glanced at the clock. "And I have to pick up some items for the craft fair. We've got a lot to do in the next week and a half if we're going to be ready." She sighed. "But all those boxes aren't going to shelve themselves once I figure this out."

Willa felt sorry for Eleanor. She wondered if she should have let Aaron take Maggie home and sorted the inventory herself, but suddenly she had a thought. She turned to Aaron, who was hovering near a stool at the end of the island waiting for his coffee. "How are you with numbers?" she asked.

He blinked. "What's that?"

Willa put out her hand to Eleanor, opening and closing it. "Let's have a look."

Eleanor frowned but passed the yellow and white sheets of paper to her. Willa carried them to Aaron and spread them out in front of him. "Do you think you could make sense of this? We check what the paperwork says was delivered against what was *actually* delivered, and then everything gets shelved in the storage room."

"Or put out front on the shelves if we're low on stock." Jane set down a white mug of steaming coffee in front of Aaron. "I hope those new measuring spoons came in because they're flying off the shelves."

"What do you think?" Willa asked Aaron, tapping one of the sheets. "This make sense to you?"

He hesitated, then glanced down. "If you're asking me if I understand how inventory works—" he shrugged "—I do." He glanced at a couple of sheets, shuffling through them. "Looks straightforward enough, but these need to be arranged by the vendor. Otherwise, you'll spend too much time reconciling what was delivered by who."

"You have experience with this?" Eleanor asked.

He nodded, not looking up. "Yes." He hesitated before going on. "My father owned a large cattle operation. I did the books for him, including keeping track of purchases, what was used, lost or damaged."

"Would you be willing to take care of this today?" Eleanor studied him. "Since nothing's going to get done outside? I'd pay you," she added quickly.

He looked at her, surprise on his face. And interest. "You would?"

"The same as Jack pays you an hour. Plus lunch and supper if it takes that long. And as many cinnamon rolls as you can eat," Eleanor added.

Willa chuckled at her sister's humor. "Maggie could stay and make ornaments with me while you work. We're having a fundraiser here next week and selling handmade crafts, cookies, homemade soup and such."

"I don't know." He hesitated. "Let me see how much inventory we're talking about here."

Eleanor pointed. "Down the hall. You probably saw some boxes as you came in, but they're also stacked in the storage room. The room's a bit of a mess. I haven't had time to sort things in weeks."

"I'll have a look," Aaron said and headed for the hall.

Eleanor made eye contact with Willa, widening her eyes. She obviously wanted her to do something, but Willa didn't know what.

"Go on," Eleanor whispered, tilting her head in the direction he'd gone. "See if he's really okay with this. He doesn't have to do it if he doesn't want to. We wouldn't want him to feel obliged."

Willa studied Aaron's broad back as he entered the hall. "But he probably needs the money," she mused softly so he wouldn't hear. She was thinking of the state of Maggie's clothing.

"Probably does. And we could use the help." Eleanor pressed her hand to her forehead. "I honestly don't know how we'll make it through the holidays at the rate we're going. We're all already working so hard. And I can't be there for Jon and keep up with work here at the store, too." Her last words were shaky.

Willa rubbed Eleanor's arm to comfort her. "You're right. We can use all the help we can get right now. I'll talk to him. I'll take care of this."

Eleanor looked at her. "You will?"

"*Ya.* Don't look so surprised." Willa tried not to be offended. She had a bit of a reputation in the family for spending much time socializing, mostly with boys, but she was a hard worker like everyone else. "I can handle this. You run your errands. And drop *Dat* off here when you leave. No need to take him with you but you know he'll get into trouble if he's left alone in the house."

The day before their father had decided to paint the downstairs bathroom door. However, he'd only gotten as far as taking the door off its hinges before he lost interest. Henry planned to rehang it before she returned home later. "*Dat* can help us make ornaments or I'll put him to work dusting shelves." Willa crossed the kitchen to follow Aaron.

"What's Papa doing?" Maggie went to the hallway entrance. "Do I have to leave?" she asked Willa.

"I'll find out," Willa answered cheerfully. "And while I do, you better try one of Jane's cinnamon rolls."

"And hot chocolate, too?"

"One hot chocolate with a big marshmallow coming up," Jane sang from the far side of the room.

Maggie scurried off and Willa went to find

Aaron. She found him standing in the doorway to the storage room.

"This is a mess," he muttered.

They stared at the disorganized boxes stacked halfway to the ceiling. Many were open with items pulled from them. Several boxes had tumbled from the weight, dumping things onto the floor.

She picked up a set of plastic mixing bowls and gingerly put them back in a box. "When we came up with the idea of building a store, we had no idea it would be so successful. Folks from all over Kent County shop here—Amish, English, Mennonite. We weren't exactly prepared, I guess."

He looked down at her. "Then maybe you should have thought through things a little better? Maybe not trying to go in so many directions at once? You're selling homemade baked goods, to-go meals, pet supplies, kitchen goods." He shook his head. "Along with horse halters and flea spray?"

She didn't like the tone of his voice. He was criticizing them and it made her angry because this dream that had become a reality had been their financial salvation. Before they opened it, they weren't sure they could continue putting food on the table. During their mother's illness, their father had begun suffering from memory loss and had been forced to quit his job. At first, all the sisters had done what they could to bring money in by sewing, selling baked goods and such. Henry had even started her own house repair business, helping widowed women. Eventually, Eleanor concluded they needed a more dependable income to run the farm and keep up with their father's medical bills. That's when they decided to build a general store on their property.

"If you don't want to do this, that's not a problem. We'll make out just fine without your help," Willa snapped. "Just leave Maggie here and go back to your sad motel room." She snatched the inventory pages out of his hand.

He lowered his head, looking directly into her eyes. "I am *not* leaving my daughter. Not anywhere. Not *ever* again," he told her from between gritted teeth. "You have no idea what she's been through. What *we've* been through."

His tone made her immediately regret her rash words. This wasn't an angry man, she realized, feeling foolish for not having seen it sooner. This was an injured man. Possibly a depressed one. Her eyes suddenly felt scratchy and she fought not to tear up. Not because he had hurt her feelings speaking so brusquely but because she had missed all the signs of a person in need.

"*Nay*, I don't know what you've been through," she said softly, meeting his gaze. "Tell me."

He walked away, shaking the paperwork. "If I'm going to do this, I do it alone. And without interruption. You got that?"

"Got it," she murmured, her heart breaking for him.

Chapter Four

Aaron stood alone in the Koffman kitchen watching rain splatter on the windowpanes. It was nearly 8:00 p.m. and well past time to return to the motel, but Maggie was in the store's salesroom. She was helping Jane and Willa tidy up the shelves of fresh baked goods so they'd be ready for sale in the morning. It was the third time she'd attempted to delay their departure and he wanted to put his foot down, but he hadn't been able to do it. Maggie was having too good a time helping. Wasn't that what a father wanted? A cheerful child willing to think of others and not just herself? Of course, he knew she benefited by being included by the Koffman sisters, but nothing was wrong with that. It was human nature to seek pleasure that also pleased others, wasn't it?

Despite worrying that it would soon be past Maggie's bedtime, he was enjoying a few minutes to himself. There hadn't been many since they left South America a month ago. It was nice to take some time to wade through his thoughts and put them neatly in their compartments in his mind. And he sure had a lot of them.

He'd had a day so pleasant that it unsettled him. He wasn't used to any happiness that didn't center on his daughter. The morning had started poorly with the rain and his fear of losing precious dollars from his projected paycheck. But the Koffman women had swept in like busy bees and given him a purpose and cash to put in his pocket after a day of work for them. It was all thanks to Willa; it had been her idea to hire him, giving him and Maggie a place to spend a rainy day other than that dreadful motel room. They'd fed him and Maggie, too. There had been a hot lunch of grilled cheese sandwiches and tomato soup with more cookies than either should have eaten. And then later Willa had convinced him to stay for supper.

Like lunch, the meal around the island in the kitchen had been full of laughter, teasing and tasty food. The sisters had thrown a supper together from leftovers in the massive commercial refrigerator of cold fried chicken, baked macaroni and cheese, a green salad, and sourdough bread. Brownies, hot from the oven with scoops of homemade vanilla ice cream, rounded out the meal. During lunch he'd been quiet, concentrating on eating and considering how he would tackle the storage room. He'd spent the morning making sense of the inventory sheets provided with the deliveries and making two calls to track down missing items the Koffmans had been charged for. He'd not been rude to Willa, but after she'd attempted to engage him in conversation of a personal nature several times, she'd left him alone. The strange thing was that as he watched her and her sisters Jane and Henry and their friend Annie converse as they ate, he'd found himself wanting to comment. It was a revelation to realize he wanted to be included.

By supper, he was pleased with his day's work and feeling more relaxed than he had in a long time. He'd met the Koffman sister Millie, her husband, Elden, and their newborn twins when they came for supper at the store. Felty Koffman, the girls' father, had been there, too. Aaron had recognized at once that the elder Koffman was suffering from Alzheimer's. Aaron knew the telltale signs because his grandfather, diagnosed with dementia, had lived with his family when he was a boy. It was a terrible disease that, like Felty, had struck his namesake too young. But Aaron had learned so much from his *grossdadi*, even in his last days when the man no longer knew his grandchildren's names or even his own. Seeing Willa and her sisters with their father, protecting him while allowing him to do what he could to be a part of the family, was admirable. Willa was patient with Felty, so sweet but teasing at the same time, which both father and daughter seemed to enjoy.

Seeing how Willa was with her family and Maggie made Aaron ashamed of how he'd behaved with her. Why had he had such a negative reaction to her? He supposed that his initial response the first day he'd met her had been based on his desire to protect Maggie. And maybe himself. It had been his experience that when people offered something, they wanted something in return. He had seen firsthand that ulterior motives could be disguised as acts of kindness. Even from friends and family. Bad motives. Manipulative ones.

Willa's gorgeous face hadn't helped in forming his first impression of her. Another preconceived notion. In the compound where he and his family had lived, the pretty women were the ones who had been the most calculating. They were groomed as spies and rewarded for the tales they told on others. The slender Willa was prettier than any of them with her heart-shaped face, big brown eyes and golden blond hair tucked neatly beneath her prayer *kapp*...

Suddenly realizing what it was about Willa that puzzled him, he reached out to grasp the window frame. He stared unseeing through the glass, closing his eyes. This tightness in his chest, the way his thoughts had been dwelling on her for days, wasn't because he had disliked her—it was because he was attracted to her.

This understanding sent him reeling. Not once since the bishop and deacons had matched him with his Ancke had he felt this way for a woman. They'd been happy together in the six months they'd courted before marriage and the four years they'd been wed before she passed. And since her death, the thought of marrying again had made him physically ill. It had been one of the reasons his father, the bishop and deacons, and the other men and women of the community had been angry with him. Three months after his wife's death he'd been notified that he'd been matched again and that the wedding would occur a month later. When he'd refused to meet with the young woman, that was when the threats began. That was when he was warned he could lose his daughter if—

"Aaron? Are you *oll recht*?"

"Are you all right?" Willa repeated in English, realizing she'd spoken partially in Pennsylvania *Deitsch*. It was the language of the

Amish, the first every child in an Old Order community learned and the one she fell back to. Children often didn't learn to speak English until they went to school.

When she entered the kitchen, he stood looking out the window, but at the sound of her voice, he'd whipped around as if startled. Or had been slapped.

Studying his face that surprisingly seemed handsome to her tonight, he *looked* like he'd been slapped. His tawny skin had taken a reddish tone and his brown eyes were wide with disbelief.

Concerned, she approached him, her footsteps echoing on the wide oak floorboards in the quiet kitchen. Behind her, from the storefront, she heard Jane and Maggie talking. "Are you okay?" she asked Aaron again.

"I—I," he stammered.

She stopped in front of him, trying to figure out what was happening. He'd been reserved much of the day, particularly with her, but at supper he'd seemed to loosen up a bit. He had chatted with her father and brother-in-law Elden, and even laughed at Jane's story about an English customer asking if the dozen fresh eggs she'd purchased needed to be boiled to make them safe. Aaron had seemed more relaxed, even appreciative of Willa when she'd asked if it would be okay to give Maggie some single-serve hot chocolate packets to take with her so she could have hot chocolate in their motel room. They made them up routinely to give away for free to customers, much like some businesses gave out lollipops.

Aaron pressed the heel of his hand to his forehead.

Something was going on with him. He was distressed, but Willa wasn't sure what to do. He'd made it clear he didn't appreciate questions, but how could she help if she didn't know what was wrong? Right now he looked like a man who needed to talk. "Do you want to sit down for a minute?" she asked him, indicating one of the stools at the center island.

He looked at the stool, hesitated, then walked to it.

She followed and sat next to him. While her first impulse was to ask again if he was okay, she forced herself to sit quietly and wait. She was rewarded when he cleared his throat. He met her gaze for a split second and then shifted his focus to his large hands on the table. They were nice hands: clean with well-trimmed nails. Strong hands.

"You asked me to tell you what we'd gone through." He spoke so softly that she had to lean closer to hear him.

He cleared his throat again. “I… We…” He exhaled and clasped his hands together as if in prayer. But Maggie told her they didn’t go to church anymore. Not since they left Paraguay.

“We lived in a Mennonite community in South America.” He spoke slowly, his voice breathy. “Well, loosely connected to the Mennonite Church. Our bishop was excommunicated for going against the teachings of the—” He stopped short. “That doesn’t matter,” he said, shaking his head. “Anyway, my wife and I were members. Both our families were. As soon as we married, we started talking, in private, about leaving the community. We started saving money from what little we had. Neither of us approved of how things were run and how far we thought we’d moved away from scripture. There were so many things going on that were so…wrong.”

She wanted to ask what kind of wrongs but stayed quiet and listened.

“Then we found out we were going to have a baby,” he continued. “And Ancke didn’t want to leave her mother and sisters. Not when she knew that we’d never see them again. That they’d never *want* to see us again once we left. So, we decided to wait.”

He went silent. When a minute ticked loudly by on the wall clock, then another, Willa gently said, "I can't imagine leaving your family after just having a new baby. Your first baby. Millie lives across the street." She smiled. "And Eleanor says we see more of her now than when she lived with us. There's comfort in being surrounded by your loved ones when you're a new mother. And a new father, too, I suspect," she added.

He nodded but still didn't look at her. "I understood, I did. And even though I couldn't stand being there, I didn't push her. We thought we'd wait until Maggie was a little older, but then—"

He gripped his hands tightly and Willa had the urge to cover them with hers. She refrained. She was an unmarried Amish woman. Amish women didn't touch men and certainly not Englishers. Or whatever he was now.

"Then Ancke got sick. Cancer. And—" His voice caught in his throat and he went quiet again. Another minute clicked by in the quiet kitchen before he picked up where he'd left off. "Maggie was still so young when Ancke died. I barely had a chance to catch my breath when our bishop, my family and the community started pressuring me to marry a woman who had been chosen for me. Without my knowledge."

Most of the kitchen lights had been turned off but in the soft lamplight of the overheads above the sink, she saw his brow furrow. It was as if he was trying to figure something out that didn't make sense to him. "She was seventeen years old, Willa. I was twenty-seven with a child. Who does that to their daughter?" he ground out angrily.

Having no reply, Willa only shook her head, fearing she might cry. But she refused to let her tears flow. She couldn't cry because her task right now was to listen to Aaron. To be strong for him. When her mother died, she learned to be strong for her sisters and *dat*.

When Aaron said nothing more, she contemplated asking him a question. He hadn't been receptive to her questions that day or earlier in the week, but by the sounds of Jane and Maggie out front, she suspected they were finishing the restocking and would return to the kitchen soon. She had to say something, didn't she? And maybe he wanted her to.

Nervous, she laid her hand beside his. Not touching it, but very close. "Is that why you and Maggie left? Because you didn't want to get married again?"

He looked at her, suddenly stony-eyed. "We left—we *fled*—because the church was trying to take my Maggie from me, and my parents were helping them. Because I had been deemed *unfit*." The last word came out in a growl. "So, I've had enough of churches."

She drew back in horror. She wasn't so naive as to think that all children belonged with their birth parents. Amish communities had the same social problems as Englishers, though not as many. Some parents *were* unfit. But even though she'd only known Aaron a few days, she knew he wasn't one of them. "Why did they think you were unfit, Aaron?" she blurted.

"Because unmarried men shouldn't have females in their household."

"But you're her *father*."

He didn't say anything.

She thought for a moment. "The church was still trying to force you into marrying again, I guess? But they wouldn't have taken Maggie from you, would they?"

He wiped his mouth with the back of his hand as if to get a sour taste from his mouth. "At first, I didn't think so, but then this widowed guy I knew, they took all three of his children when he refused to remarry and gave them to another family. His son and two daughters."

Unable to sit any longer, she jumped up from her stool. "That's not legal!"

"We were living where laws didn't matter much," he said dully. "We were left alone."

"But what about God's laws?" she asked.

He crossed his arms over his chest, turning to her. "I asked that a lot in the beginning. When we first got there. I was a fourteen-year-old boy. I had a lot of questions. But I was punished often enough to stop asking them."

She wanted to ask how he'd been punished but didn't dare. Instead, she asked, "Why did you and Maggie come here? To an Amish community? Was it because of your uncle?"

He shrugged. "I didn't know anyone else, anywhere. I hadn't seen Jessop and Sissy for at least two years before we packed up and moved from Pennsylvania to South America. So…almost sixteen years." He stared at the floorboards. "He and my father had a terrible falling-out. Jessop hadn't been angry when my father decided to leave the Amish Church, but when—"

"Wait," she said, trying not to sound or look too shocked. "You used to be Amish?"

He nodded. "Until I was twelve. We had a big dairy farm in a community north of Lancaster. Then my *dat* met Bishop Terrence and we became Mennonite, and two years later…"

He didn't finish so she finished for him. "You all moved to Paraguay."

He nodded, quiet again.

"Ach." Willa took a step toward him. "Aaron, I am so sorry. Please tell me what I can do to—"

"Papa! Papa!" Maggie burst into the kitchen. "Look what Jane gave me!" She waved a wooden spoon in each hand. "Spoons to stir our soup!

You said we needed a wooden spoon and I got two!"

Aaron rose, wiping a hand across his eyes. "We're not taking the Koffmans' spoons. They can sell those in their store."

The lights visible in the kitchen from the customer area of the store went out and Jane walked into the kitchen. "It's fine, Aaron. They're a gift to Maggie. Someone opened the package and one spoon is missing so we can't sell the pack. She's welcome to them." She looked down at Maggie. "And she did so much work today that I feel she deserves more than a couple of spoons."

"Fine," Aaron said. He looked at Maggie. "All right, bring your spoons and let's go. Jane and Willa have to be back here in the morning. And hopefully, I do, too." He glanced in the direction of the dark window. "Though the weather's not looking too promising."

"Come in the morning anyway." Willa crossed the kitchen and headed toward the back door. "If there's no work outside, we've got plenty here for you to do."

Aaron laid a hand on Maggie's shoulder and steered her in the same direction. "I can't ask you to find another day's work for me."

Jane laughed. "There's no *finding* to it. There's plenty to do. And we need the help, Aaron. You'd be doing us a favor."

"You would," Willa agreed. "Eleanor is doing too much and the coming week will be crazier than usual because of the craft fair."

"I'll think about it," Aaron said. "Good night, Jane."

"Night!" she called cheerfully, then sang, "See you in the morning, Maggie."

"See you in the morning, Jane," Maggie responded in delight.

In the hall, Willa took down Maggie's coat and hat and the little girl let her help her put them on. Meanwhile, Aaron slipped on his coat.

Willa crouched to hand Maggie her spoons and zip up her coat.

"See you in the morning," Maggie said with a big grin.

Willa looked over the girl's shoulder at her father. "I hope so. Those dough ornaments we made today should be ready for some polyurethane spray to seal them. Then we just have to put the ribbons through them and they're ready to be sold."

"Ready, Maggie Mae?" Aaron asked, pulling his watch cap down low over his ears.

"Ready!" Maggie declared, opening the door. Then she spun around. "But, Papa, what about our stuff? The cookies and hot chocolate Willa gave us?"

"Already in the car," he told her.

Willa held open the door for them, feeling awkward. She'd never had such an intense conversation with someone she didn't know well and wasn't sure exactly what to do with all she'd learned. She supposed she'd have to see how he responded and go on from there. She wished they hadn't been interrupted because she felt the conversation could have gone further. But maybe they'd talked enough for him for one night. Maybe too much.

Aaron followed Maggie out the door but stopped before he stepped onto the stoop. He surprised Willa by turning around and making eye contact. "Thank you," he said softly. "For everything today. Tonight."

She smiled up at him, feeling strangely warm. Looking into his eyes made her feel off-kilter. What it was, she didn't know. "Of course. And please come back tomorrow, even if it is raining. We're terribly worried about Eleanor. About her health. She can't keep burning the candle at both ends."

"We'll see," he said, glancing out the door as Maggie clattered down the steps. He looked back at Willa. "Maybe it will clear up and Mark will expect me to work."

"Maybe," she agreed. However, she'd overheard Elden telling Millie that it was supposed to rain again all day.

"Maybe," he repeated. "Well...good night."

"Guder nacht," she answered.

Aaron grasped the door handle to close it behind him but stopped halfway out the door and turned back again. "Willa?"

"Ya?" He looked tired, but she also thought he looked better. At least better than he had when they'd been talking alone in the kitchen. It made her feel good to think that maybe she had relieved some of his burden by listening to him.

He glanced at the floor. "I'd... I'd appreciate it—if you did not repeat what I told you. Not to anyone." He lifted his gaze. "I... I shouldn't have gone on like that. Troubled you that way."

"Of course I won't say anything," she said. "I'm so sorry for what you and Maggie have been through. But I'm glad you told me. Sometimes the best way to lighten a load is to share it. That's what our *mam* used to say."

He nodded and then the most beautiful thing happened. Aaron smiled at her and then he was gone.

Willa stared at the closed door realizing that this feeling she'd been getting all day, all week, was attraction. An attraction she'd never experienced deep inside like this. How tragic, she thought. She was Amish and he wasn't.

They could never marry.

Chapter Five

Willa pushed a shopping cart down the baking aisle of Byler's store in search of blue-and-white jimmies. She wanted them for the sugar cookies she and Maggie planned to make the following day, meaning she needed several cups of each color. The little girl begged to come to the store with her and Annie, but Willa insisted she remain with Jane. There was no way Willa would ask Aaron if she could take Maggie to town, not after what he had told her the previous week about his parents and church trying to take her from him. Aaron now trusted Willa and her sisters with Maggie as long as they kept the child near him. But Willa understood the remnants of the fear he still held and knew it would take time for it to fade.

As she scanned the shelf looking at bags of green-and-red sprinkles, Willa's mind returned to thoughts of Aaron. Since their talk in the kitchen the previous week, she spent more time reflecting on him than she cared to admit. She vacillated between thinking about his awful experiences in South America and her inexplicable attraction to him. Her fascination with him made no sense. He was nothing like the men she'd dated or flirted with before. He didn't act like any of them. He wasn't carefree. He certainly wasn't even-tempered and always up for a good time. He was older and didn't have the striking good looks of the boys she liked to be seen with. And most importantly, he wasn't Amish. Aaron didn't attend church anywhere. He wasn't a man she could date or marry, which meant neither her family nor church would approve of him as a suitor. She knew he could never be a suitor, but she couldn't control the irrational thoughts swirling in her mind.

She wondered why she thought he was handsome now when she'd thought the opposite the first time she saw him. Why did she watch him when he wasn't looking? Why did she purposely choose to wear her prettiest dresses to work at the store? And why did she lie in bed at night going over the conversations she'd had with him that day? Their exchanges were mostly about Maggie, but sometimes they chatted when passing each other in the kitchen when he came in for lunch. They had not had a private conversation since that night in the kitchen, but she found herself hanging on to his every word. And she couldn't stop thinking about him even though she knew she shouldn't. She didn't *want* to. Aaron Raber was a man forbidden to her.

"Got 'em."

Willa glanced up, startled. She had been so lost in thought that she hadn't seen her friend Annie coming down the aisle.

"Sorry it took so long." Annie set an armful of sub sandwiches in the cart. She was a pretty girl in her midtwenties with brown hair, green eyes and a smile that lit up a room. "Long line for this time of morning." They'd decided to get Italian subs for lunch for everyone working at the store because they had no leftovers and wouldn't have time to cook anything by the time they returned in the buggy. Annie's brow furrowed. "What are you looking for? I know you're working on cookies for Saturday's fundraiser, but can't you use the supplies you sell in the store?"

Feeling guilty for being caught dwelling on Aaron, Willa turned to the shelves. "*Ach.* We usually do, especially now that we're buying some ingredients in bulk and rebagging them. But not everything I need is something we sell. I'm looking for blue-and-white jimmies for frosted sugar cookies we'll cut in the shape of stars. I can't find them." She shrugged. "I guess we can make them with what we have but I wanted to sell something that wasn't red and green."

Annie looked questioningly at Willa and slowly reached in front of her, removing a big bag of mixed blue-and-white jimmies from the eye-level shelf.

Flustered, Willa grabbed them from her and retrieved another bag from the shelf. "Silly me. I don't know how I missed them." She put them in the cart, feeling overheated suddenly. Like Annie, she was dressed for town in a long black wool cloak and her black wool bonnet worn over her prayer *kapp.* "I don't know where my head is."

Annie raised an eyebrow. "Maybe with the handsome employee you were chatting up this morning?"

Willa drew back, covering her embarrassment with a laugh. "I was not *chatting up* Aaron." She grimaced. "And who said he was handsome?" She lowered her gaze as an elderly English woman in a puffy white coat walked past them carrying a gallon of milk. If anyone from Honeycomb saw them making a spectacle of themselves in the store, word was sure to get back to her aunt Judy. She waited until the stranger was out of earshot before she leaned over their cart and harshly whispered, "I never said Aaron was good-looking."

"But he is, isn't he?" Annie teased.

Willa leaned closer to Annie to hiss, "You shouldn't be saying such things. He's an Englisher!"

"Not exactly." Her friend smiled mischievously. "Eleanor told me he used to be Mennonite and before that, Amish."

"Who told Eleanor that?" Willa asked with surprise. She'd taken care not to share anything Aaron had said that night alone in the kitchen. She'd done so not just because he'd specifically asked her not to but she wanted to protect him and Maggie from wagging tongues and judgments.

"He did, I guess." Annie got behind the cart and pushed it forward. "If he falls in love with you, he could always become Amish again and marry you."

Willa felt herself blush and grabbed a bag of rye flour as they walked past a display. "Take my word for it, he's not going to become Amish again."

"It's happened," Annie insisted. "My cousin had a friend in Wisconsin who married a man who left during his *rumspringa* and returned years later. They moved to another state to make a new start together."

Willa added the flour to the cart and kept walking. "I am not marrying an Englisher, Annie, and I'm not leaving Honeycomb. Not ever."

"I'm just saying there are possibilities. You said Eleanor's lost her patience with you because you haven't found a husband. Wouldn't it be better to marry a man you know than one a matchmaker chooses for you?"

Willa glanced over her shoulder, wondering if Annie knew that her father was thinking about hiring a matchmaker to find a husband for *her*. She decided she wouldn't say anything. At least not today. She let Annie push the cart past her and walked beside her. The flour was the last item they'd come for and they made their way toward the busy cash registers. "Can we not talk about Aaron Raber?"

Annie leaned closer and whispered in her ear. "You know he watches you when you're not looking."

Willa grabbed Annie's arm, resisting a smile of pleasure. "He does not."

"Does, too. Yesterday at lunch, you got up to get more butter from the fridge and I saw him watching you cross the room. And Saturday morning, when I was looking for those new fancy rolling pins in the storage room, he was stalling in the hallway pretending to look at a piece of paper when he was waiting for you because I said you needed more paper bags."

Willa thought for a moment, replaying that encounter in the hallway with Aaron. She'd been headed for the storeroom and he had been standing there looking at a yellow receipt from one of their vendors. When she came down the hall, he'd smiled at her and asked whether she thought they should order more dark brown sugar because of how fast they were going through the last case.

The idea that he might have been waiting for her made Willa smile before she could catch herself.

"Aha!" Annie exclaimed. "You *do* think he's handsome."

"We're not talking about this anymore. About him," Willa said, flustered again. She grabbed the front of the cart and took the lead, pulling it as she tried to push thoughts of Aaron from her mind.

Of course, it didn't work. The more she tried *not* to think about him, the more she did.

He likes me, she thought. Against her will, a little trill of happiness went through her and made her smile again.

Aaron nodded to his two Amish coworkers as he jumped down from the addition where they were laying subfloor. It had been a long morning, one he mostly spent carrying heavy plywood for the crew and trying not to get in their way. He had known from day one that he wouldn't like construction work, but he wasn't good at it, either. The men he worked with didn't seem to care because he was a hard worker, but he did. While he appreciated Willa's brother-in-law's willingness to give him a job for as long as he needed it, he needed to find another. One he was better suited to. Sunday afternoon, he'd started his search, perusing the want ads of a local free paper.

It had been a long, dismal day in the motel. The rain from the week before had continued through the afternoon and Maggie had grumbled nonstop about wanting to be at the Koffman store. He kept thinking the same thing but hadn't admitted it to his daughter. Thankfully, because it was Sunday, he could honestly say they couldn't go because the Amish didn't work on Sundays.

Due to the rain, he'd worked again Friday for the Koffmans inside the store and then, he'd ended up working half a day on Saturday. He'd not planned to return over the weekend, but he and Maggie had stopped by because she left her hat there. While he was chatting with Willa, Eleanor had asked him if there was any way he could stay a few hours. She needed someone to organize and inventory the apartment's living area over the store they used for extra storage until the addition was completed. Beth and her husband, Jack, had recently vacated the apartment when they moved into their new house next door. It was the perfect temporary spot for overflow because it was on-site but out of the way. Aaron had happily agreed and put in four hours while Maggie made herself useful downstairs "helping" Willa at the cash register and dusting store shelves.

With the unexpected wages for Saturday, Aaron had more money than he'd budgeted for, and he and Maggie had gone to a restaurant for pizza—a new experience for them both. That was where he'd picked up the free paper to look for jobs. He liked what he had done the last few days at the Koffman store and wondered if he could find a job doing something like that. He imagined Eleanor would even be okay with him using her as a reference.

Lem, the taller of the two Amish men, nodded as Aaron walked by, headed for the Koffman kitchen and the lunch he imagined was waiting for him. Lem and his cousin Rufus were leaning against the tailgate of Mark's pickup, waiting for him. Mark had gone inside to see Eleanor forty-five minutes ago, leaving them to wrap up the morning's work. Sometimes the guys came inside to warm up and eat while he had lunch with Maggie, but they often ran into Dover for fast food. Aaron didn't have money for burgers and fries and milkshakes, but even if he did, he preferred to eat with his daughter in the store kitchen. And the meal was better.

When he entered the back door, Aaron was surprised not to find Maggie waiting for him. On previous days, when he came inside, she raced down the hall to throw herself into his arms. Curious about where she was, he wiped his feet on the floor mat as he removed his hat and coat. Rubbing his hands together to warm them, he listened for his daughter's voice but didn't hear her. A week ago, he would have instantly been concerned where she was. But now, after spending a few days with Willa and her sisters, he'd lost his fear that they had any ulterior motives concerning Maggie. They had no intention of taking her away from him.

Voices drifted into the hall from the kitchen. He heard Eleanor, Willa and Mark. He couldn't make out what they were saying, but he assumed they were discussing details of the addition. Mark had told him that the blueprint had changed several times over the summer as the business became more successful. The addition was now four hundred square feet larger than the original plan and the second story would have a storage room and small apartment.

He glanced farther down the hall toward the bathroom; the door was open so Maggie wasn't there. She was probably out front with Jane and Annie. Maybe Felty was with them, too. If he was, maybe they could have lunch together. Despite the older man's diminished abilities, Aaron still enjoyed his company. He wasn't rigid or controlling like his father had been, and he was eager for the older man's wisdom.

The thought of lunch made his stomach grumble. He had allowed Maggie to have breakfast with Willa for the last three days, but so far, he'd resisted offers of fresh eggs fried in butter, scrapple, biscuits with local honey, stacks of fluffy buttermilk pancakes and homemade sausage patties. He stepped into the bathroom to wash his hands and headed for the kitchen. As he approached, he smelled something cheesy baking and thought it might be a casserole.

Aaron walked in to find Mark, Willa and Eleanor all standing together in front of the kitchen sink with their heads together. When he entered, they went silent and looked at him. He was no fool; he knew when someone was talking about him. He nodded in their direction, feeling awkward. "Maggie around?" he asked, feeling like he had to say something because all three were as quiet as mice.

"Out front. Millie stopped by with the babies for a few minutes and, um, you know how fascinated she is with them." Willa picked up two hot mitts and opened one of the oven doors. The deliciously cheesy scent got stronger. "We made a casserole with ground beef, tomato sauce, cheddar cheese and elbow macaroni. It sells well in our ready-to-bake section. The Englishers call it Hamburger Helper." She laughed nervously.

Eleanor and Mark were still looking at him. Then Mark glanced at Eleanor and cleared his throat. "Um, I wanted to talk to you about something, Aaron."

Eleanor made herself busy pulling a cooling rack from a cabinet.

Aaron's chest tightened and a lump rose in his throat. Mark was going to fire him. The foreman knew Aaron wasn't cut out for construction work; he knew he wasn't pulling his weight and would hire someone who would. But Aaron needed this job. He hadn't even put any applications in elsewhere yet.

"We were talking and… I was wondering…" Mark slid his hands into his pockets and walked toward Aaron. "Um, if you'd consider, well, um—"

"Oh," Eleanor exclaimed, interrupting him.

She turned to Aaron. "Would you like to quit working for Mark out in the cold and rain and come inside to work for us?"

Aaron blinked, confused for a moment. "For you?"

"For the store," Mark answered. "If...if you'd be interested."

The idea excited Aaron at once. And came as a relief. He liked the work he'd been doing for the Koffmans and was good at it. And if he worked at the store, Maggie could be right here with him. He knew for a fact that employees could bring their children. Eleanor had hired a young Amish woman to work the cash register and he'd overheard her telling her that she was welcome to bring her toddler.

Aaron nodded. "I might be interested."

Mark looked relieved and pleased at the same time. "Eleanor says they really need help and you did a terrific job getting her inventory straight. And you made phone calls for her and..."

And I'm terrible with a hammer, Aaron thought.

But was it right to leave Jack hanging? He'd much rather work in the store than on the addition, but his uncle had gotten him the job and Jack had given it to him out of the goodness of his heart. It would be wrong to quit less than two weeks later, wouldn't it? He found his gaze drifting toward Willa. She pulled out the casserole, set it on the rack and stood looking at him. She didn't seem that enthusiastic, and that upset him. She had such an uplifting spirit that just being in the same room with her made him feel like maybe everything would be all right.

"When would you want me to start?" Aaron asked Eleanor.

Eleanor chuckled. "After lunch?"

Aaron looked at Mark. "And Jack would be okay with me quitting? You'd be one man down on the job. Well, at least half a man," he added. "I know I don't know what I'm doing. Jack knew it, too, when he hired me."

"He's fine with it."

"I mentioned the idea to Jack last night," Eleanor explained.

Aaron looked at Willa again. She turned away from him and began removing white plates from a drawer in a cabinet.

Aaron turned his attention to Mark. "You'd be all right with working short a man? Even if he's just your gopher?"

"We've got two guys who want to work for Jack. He can put one here and one on another job, a renovation, over Hazlettville way."

Aaron nodded. "And exactly what would I be doing here?"

Eleanor shrugged. "Same as you've been doing.

But more," she added quickly. "I've got a whole list of things that need to be done by Friday afternoon so we can be ready for the craft fair on Saturday. Phone calls to make, tables to be picked up." She pressed her hand to her forehead. "And I have to watch Emmy and Jamie all day Friday for Jon. He has furniture he made to deliver and set up for some Englishers north of Smyrna." She dropped her hand. "Oh, and I'll raise your hourly pay."

"You don't need to do that," Aaron told her. "Your payment has been fair for the hours I put in. More than enough."

Eleanor shook her head. "I insist. I've found that better pay gets me better employees. I need someone I can trust with the tasks I'm responsible for. Not just inventory but work schedules, payroll and bookkeeping. Willa, Jane and the others are too busy minding the store, baking and making for the Christmas season. I can't ask them to do any more." Her tone softened. "It would be a huge help to us all, Aaron. Right now, you seem like a gift from *Gott*."

Not hardly, he thought. He had been excommunicated from his church. He had no real job and he was living in a motel. But he didn't say that. Instead, he glanced at Willa, saw that she was watching him and nodded his assent. "All right, I'll take the job here." He raised a finger. "But only through the holiday season."

"And then we can reassess," Eleanor declared quickly.

"And I need a description of duties written down," Aaron warned. "I don't mind if you add tasks day to day, but I want an idea of what I'm expected to do. I like to plan and have duties laid out in a logical sequence. It's more efficient."

"Absolutely." Eleanor beamed.

"Well." Mark clapped his hands together loudly. "That's that. So, me and the boys are going to run into Dover. I'll get a check to you for this week's work, Aaron." He headed for the back door.

"Danki!" Aaron said as he raised his hand goodbye.

"See you later, Mark." Willa didn't turn from the sink.

"I'm so glad you're going to do this for us," Eleanor told Aaron as she made a beeline for the door to the storefront. "You've just made my life so much easier. Our lives."

She left the kitchen and then it was just him and Willa. He felt awkward now. Maybe spending so much time near Willa wasn't a good idea. Because his attraction to her wasn't waning. In fact, it was getting stronger. But nothing had changed. There wouldn't be even a remote possibility that he could pursue the temptation. He couldn't be Amish again; it was a poor fit at this stage of his life. He didn't think he could ever be anything again.

"Congratulations," Willa said, her voice soft in the quiet room. "You'll be a lot of help to Eleanor. To us," she added.

She carried a clean dish to a cupboard and was now standing an arm's length away from him. He felt something akin to a buzz of energy as she met his gaze. And then he saw something in her brown eyes that told him she was feeling the same way he was.

Had he made a terrible mistake accepting this job?

Chapter Six

On the day of the benefit for the Coblenz family, Willa paused in the doorway to watch the flurry of activity. The store was full of Englishers, all smiles and chatter, cheerfully making craft and food purchases. Insisting it was for a good cause, Jane had borrowed a CD player from a Mennonite friend. Though music wasn't allowed in an Amish home or church service, Christmas carols played from the tinny speaker. And while it wasn't Thanksgiving yet, the Advent season had come early to the Koffman store. Their brothers-in-law had put a huge balsam wreath decorated with pinecones and holly berries on the front door. They'd also placed fresh-cut pine boughs around the store, and the scent, mixed with clove and cinnamon potpourri bubbling on the woodstove, made the whole place smell like the Christmas holidays were already upon them.

"Oh, come all ye faithful," Willa sang softly

along with the music. It was a song she knew well because they had been singing it in church for as long as she could remember.

She was pleased that the fundraiser would be even more successful than she anticipated. Because the day was sunny, the temperature brisk but not cold, Eleanor was able to put several sales tables on the front porch, leaving more room for customers to walk around inside. The displays were laden with homemade Christmas crafts and cookies, canned goods from Amish gardens and handmade gifts like wooden toys and quilted pillow covers. Eleanor had astonishingly managed to have every item donated so Willa was confident that Jon could pay off the remainder of his late wife's massive medical bills. Then he could move on to the next stage of his life. And it was all because her big sister recognized that because Old Amish didn't have insurance, without help from his community, he might have spent the remainder of his life paying off what he owed.

When Eleanor realized how many donations they had, she became concerned there wouldn't be enough help to run the store and man the fundraiser tables simultaneously. However, they ended up with more volunteers than they knew what to do with. Not only did a dozen women from their Amish community bring their donations early that morning, but most stayed to pitch in. Mark and Rosie Miller even showed up, bringing several women from the Mennonite church they attended. Eleanor put Rosie in charge of the soups and sandwiches to go, and she and her friends filled the kitchen with laughter as they prepared preorders and kept the tables stocked out front. Meanwhile, Mark and Aaron oversaw the parking because the store's gravel lot had quickly overflowed, and cars were parking on the road and lining up and down the driveway that led to the Koffman home behind the store.

"Coming through!" Jane called from behind Willa. "Beep, beep!"

Willa stepped out of the way as her little sister approached with a tray of quart containers filled with homemade roasted butternut squash soup.

As Jane passed, she asked, "Did you ever find those paper napkins I asked for?"

"Ach." Willa rolled her eyes. "Sorry. I've been running myself ragged, trying to be sure everyone has what they need. Annie ran out of bags at the register, Millie couldn't find the bales of twine we sell and our dear aunt requested I fetch hot tea for her three times. And last time Judy grilled me about when I would do my duty and marry."

Her maternal aunt was married to their bishop and had always been a thorn in their mother's side. She had not been blessed with children but always had plenty of opinions on how her sister should raise hers. With Willa's mother gone, Judy now focused on criticizing Eleanor's choices as head of the Koffman household and annoying her other nieces.

Willa breathed deeply, settling herself. "I didn't forget the napkins you needed, Jane," she continued. "I couldn't find them. I checked both the storeroom and upstairs where Aaron moved the supplies and didn't see them."

Jane frowned. "Look again. We're nearly out." She headed toward the front of the store where the Mennonite women were selling the containers of homemade soup as fast as they could be brought out from the back. "And spoons!"

Willa made a face. "What do customers need spoons for?"

"I don't know." Jane shrugged, pulling the tray closer so a customer didn't bump into it. "To eat it in their cars?"

Willa laughed. "Cold soup?"

"Maybe they're eating Annie's bread pudding!" Jane waited for a break in the line of folks strolling by as they checked out the craft tables before she stepped into the fray.

Willa called after her over the sounds of the Christmas music playing and the voices of the customers. "But, Jane—"

"Ask Aaron!" Jane shouted as she disappeared into the crowd of jostling customers. "You can never find anything!"

"*Oll recht, oll recht.* Fine. I'll ask Aaron," Willa muttered under her breath.

He and Maggie had arrived at 7:00 a.m. that morning to help set up the tables and assist with the fundraiser in whatever capacity needed. It had been sweet of him to volunteer, but Willa couldn't help hopefully wondering if he had ulterior motives. Had he come because it was an excuse to see her? She knew she'd woken that morning looking forward to the day for that reason. It was as if the more she saw him, the more she wanted to. It was an odd feeling. She'd never experienced that with anyone before. It was interesting how quickly she'd gotten used to having him around the store now that he was working full-time for them. She looked forward every day to seeing him and Maggie. The little girl made Willa smile a dozen times a day. And as much as she hated to admit it, so did her father.

Willa didn't understand her growing attraction to Aaron. She certainly hadn't cared for him the day they met. Was it because he was forbidden so she knew it couldn't go anywhere? Was Eleanor right? Was she self-sabotaging her chances for marriage? Was that why she always set her sights on ill-suited bachelors? Did she not want to marry and have a family?

She shook her head, walking toward the storeroom to look again for the napkins before she looked for Aaron.

Of course I want to marry, she thought. *But I don't want a matchmaker choosing my husband. I want to do that myself. Is it my fault the right man hasn't come along?*

Willa was so lost in her thoughts that as she went down the hallway, she almost ran smack into who else but Aaron.

"Oh," he said cheerfully, stepping back to look at her. "Sorry."

"*Nay.* My fault." She held her palms out to him, chuckling. "I was lost in my head. Busy spinning cobwebs." She laughed again. "It was something my *mam* used to say when we were daydreaming."

"My mother used to say the same thing." He smiled at her.

It was a lingering smile she understood well from years of dating; it was a smile of attraction. She couldn't help herself; she smiled back.

"Needed my leather work gloves." He held up a worn pair. "A man parked his car a little too far off the road and his back tire slid into the ditch."

"Oh no!" She covered her mouth with her hand. "Is everyone all right?"

"The driver and his wife are fine. Apparently, she warned him he was parking wrong. That's what she told me. Several times." The edges of his mouth twitched in amusement. "I'm going to help Mark pull them out with his truck." He grimaced. "Though I think they're disappointed that we won't use an *Aim-ish* horse."

They both laughed at the common mispronunciation, an energy coursing between them that made her feel all tingly. This was a side of Aaron she had only seen glimpses of before. Today he was so animated and seemed genuinely happy.

"I've been sent in search of paper napkins." She pointed down the hall in the direction of the storeroom. "I already looked upstairs. And we need disposable spoons, too." She shrugged.

His broad brow creased. He looked nice today in a pair of Levi's jeans and a dark green plaid flannel shirt. He smelled of shampoo and shaving soap. When he'd arrived in Honeycomb he looked as if he only shaved every few days but for the last week, he'd shown up at the store every day clean-shaven. She liked his smooth face and had a nearly irresistible desire to touch it. For once, however, she was able to subdue an impulse.

"You didn't find napkins at the top of the stairs near the quart-sized plastic soup tubs?" he asked. "I thought I moved all the paper goods up there."

She shook her head.

"Hmm. Maybe there are some still in the storeroom?"

"I'll look there, too," she said, moving so she could pass him and continue down the hall.

"Why don't you wait and I'll look. They might be on the very top shelf. Too high for you. You'll need the stepladder."

"Are you saying I'm short?" she asked, giving him a sassy smile.

His brown eyes twinkled with mischief and she realized that she was flirting with an Englisher, something she'd never done in her life. Even more shocking was that Aaron was flirting back. She felt a little tremor of excitement. It was something akin to the feeling she got when she met a new potential beau. But this felt different.

"Short? Nah. You're not short, Willa. I think it's called height challenged." He smirked.

She rolled her eyes at him.

"What I was saying," he continued, "was that you're going to need a ladder." He tilted his head in the direction of the main road. “Let me give Mark a hand with that car and I’ll be right back. I’ll find them for you. I can reach the top shelf without the ladder.”

She placed her hand on her hip, her tone still good-humored. “And you think I can’t manage a ladder? Who do you think was getting things off high shelves before you started working here?”

He leaned closer, towering over her, but not in an intimidating way. “I do not think you can’t handle a ladder. In fact, Willa Koffman, I don’t think there’s a thing on earth you couldn’t handle.”

Her cheeks made warm by his compliment, she tucked her hands behind her, gazing up at him. She had to press her lips together to keep from grinning. “You’ve got that right. Our mother did not raise girls who—”

A horn beeped so nearby that it startled them both and Aaron swung the door open. It was Mark in his pickup truck. He had his window down, leaning out of it. “Aaron! You coming or not?” He gazed past him to Willa.

Feeling as if she’d be caught doing something naughty, which she had been, she stepped out of his view.

“I’m coming,” Aaron called. He said to Willa,

"Give me a few minutes. I'll be back as quick as I can."

He closed the door before she could think of a clever retort. She stared at it momentarily, trying to figure out what had transpired between them. How had they gone from a mutual dislike…to flirting? And what was wrong with her to have behaved so brazenly? She pressed her back to the door and leaned against it.

It wasn't that she'd never flirted with a boy before. But Aaron didn't fall into the same category as all the Amish boys she'd toyed with, rode home in buggies with and dated. Aaron was no boy. He was a man.

And because he wasn't Amish, he was practically an *English* man, she reminded herself sternly.

With that thought, she went in search of the stepladder. First, she checked the storeroom, but it wasn't there. Then she looked upstairs but came down empty-handed again. The last possible place she could think to hunt was the kitchen. It wasn't there, either, but she located their six-foot aluminum ladder leaning against the wall. One of her brothers-in-law probably left it when they hung the greenery that morning. She had intended to grab it and return to the storeroom just to demonstrate to Aaron that she didn't need his help, but she got waylaid by

Mark's sister Rosie. The other volunteers in the kitchen had to get to a church function and Rosie needed help. Willa spent twenty minutes filling plastic containers with chicken and dumplings.

"That's it, that's the last of it," Willa declared as she set down the ladle.

Rosie laughed. "That's the last of everything." She glanced at the clock. "And with less than an hour to go until we close shop, I think we'll sell out of all the prepared foods."

Willa's eyes grew round as she popped the last lid on. "We sold all the soup? Even Jane's corn chowder with the chili powder in it?" Her little sister was a good cook but sometimes a little too adventurous for Willa's taste.

"That was the first to go." Pleased, Rosie dried her hands on a dish towel. "Thanks for your help."

"*Nay*, thank you, Rosie." Willa threw her arms around her. "We couldn't have done all this without you, Mark and your friends. And you're not even Amish."

Rosie returned the hug. "But we worship the same God, don't we? And I know He likes to see us help others, no matter what church they attend. Or no church at all. It's as simple as that."

Willa was still thinking about what Rosie had said when she carried the ladder into the storeroom. The event was almost over, but she figured if they didn't use the napkins today, at least they would know where they were for the next time they were needed.

Aaron had organized the boxes of items sold in the store so neatly that she had no trouble placing the ladder on the floor and climbing the rungs. She found a big box of napkins on the top shelf. And beside it was half a box of plastic spoons. She must have missed them the first time because from the floor, she couldn't see the tiny writing indicating what was inside the oversize box.

Pleased to have located them on her own, she grasped the box and slid it forward. Then she looked down, realizing the box was too big to carry down the ladder. How would she hold on to the ladder with one hand and the box with the other? Feeling a bit off-balance, she exhaled nervously. Should she wait for Aaron?

But that seemed silly. She could certainly get a box down. One of her sisters had gotten it up there, hadn't they?

She looked down again and then, holding the box close, she took one tentative step down. The ladder wobbled and she leaned forward to steady herself. Apparently, she hadn't placed the ladder very well. "Whoa," she muttered and took another step down.

"What do you think you're doing?" came a voice behind her. It was Aaron.

She heard him rush forward.

"I said I'd do that," he told her. "Put it back up if you can and I'll get it."

Willa considered arguing with him, but she didn't really want to try to get the box down now. Especially because at this point, if she fell, he'd witness the whole thing. She slowly lifted the box and returned it to the shelf.

"You don't have the ladder stabilized." Aaron grasped the side rails to steady it. "Come on down. I'll get the box."

Willa didn't know why, but instead of coming down the ladder backward, she turned to face Aaron. He held both sides of the ladder as she slowly came down. His gaze met hers and she couldn't look away. When she was eye to eye with him, he still didn't remove his hands from the ladder, so his arms were around her but not touching.

She took another step and he surprised her by leaning close to brush his lips against hers.

The moment he did it, he let go of the ladder as if it were hot. "I'm sorry. I'm so sorry," he said, backing up, his hands in the air. He looked as surprised as she felt.

Willa touched her mouth with her fingertip. She felt all tingly inside and out.

He lowered his gaze as she reached solid

ground. “I’m sorry,” he repeated in anguish. “I don’t know what—”

“Aaron, it’s all right,” she said, feeling bad that he was so upset with himself. “It’s not as if it’s the first time I’ve ever been kissed,” she told him, feeling surprisingly bold now.

“I’ve never… I’m sorry,” he repeated. He grabbed the big cardboard napkin box and handed it to her.

She set it on the floor, watching him. She wasn’t upset that he’d kissed her. She’d liked it, even though she knew she shouldn’t have.

Without making eye contact, he said, “I really am sorry. I won’t let it happen again.”

Her senses returned to her and she nodded as she tried to push the feel of his mouth from her mind. He was right, of course. It could never happen again. She knew that because what she had told him was only partially true. This wasn’t the first time she’d ever been kissed. There had been others, boys she had fancied herself in love with and dreamed of marrying, at least for a few days. But no one like Aaron had ever kissed her before. No one had ever made her feel the way she felt right now.

“*Ya*, of course,” she agreed. “Never again.”

And then he hurried out of the storeroom.

Willa watched him go and all she could think was, what if I wish he would kiss me again?

* * *

Aaron burst out the back door of the store feeling as if he couldn't catch his breath. He had no idea what he had been thinking when he kissed Willa. He'd not intended that to happen. The thought had never crossed his mind. But she was practically in his arms, looking so— He'd never kissed anyone on her lips but his Ancke and that hadn't happened until they were married. What was wrong with him?

"Aaron? You okay?"

Aaron looked up to see Mark leaning against his truck, arms folded. "You look like you've seen a ghost."

Aaron walked over to stare at the partially constructed addition.

Mark's eyes were filled with concern. "What's wrong, buddy?"

"I..." Aaron wiped his mouth with the back of his hand, but it didn't take away the feel of Willa's lips on his. How could he have done such a thing? Willa Koffman was Amish. No matter how he felt about her or how strong these feelings felt right now, she was off-limits. He could never marry her, which meant he had no right to kiss her. Not ever.

"Aaron—"

Aaron glanced at Mark, then away. "I did a terrible thing," he blurted. He closed his eyes.

This wasn't like him to make confessions, but he needed to learn to start trusting people. And if anyone was trustworthy, it was Mark. "I… I don't know what happened. Willa was there and…and—" He opened his eyes. "And I kissed her."

The corners of Mark's mouth twitched as he fought a smile. "Okay," he said slowly. "So why are you so upset? Was it terrible?"

Aaron grimaced, unable to see the humor in the situation. "No, no, it was amazing, but—" He fell silent, not wanting to think about how incredible her mouth had felt against his. He felt so guilty. Almost as if he had cheated on Ancke. Logically he knew he hadn't but… But it had still been wrong.

Mark slid his hands into his jeans pockets, his tone kind but still with a hint of amusement. "Aaron, I hate to tell you this, but you're not the first to kiss Willa Koffman."

Aaron snapped his head around to look at him. "Have *you* kissed her?"

"I'm not a man to kiss and tell." Mark's mouth twitched into a playful smile. "Like…some."

Aaron brought his hand to his face again and Mark chuckled. "Aaron, it's okay," he said. "Was Willa upset with you?"

Aaron shook his head. "No. She said the same as you. But I'm confused. I thought Amish women didn't—back in my day, when I was Amish, women never—" He exhaled. "I thought kissing was only meant for married couples. Or at least betrothed."

Again, his friend chuckled. "It's supposed to be that way, but things are changing in some Amish churches. Kissing between a man and a woman who aren't married certainly isn't encouraged, but it's acknowledged that it happens. And you know Willa well enough to see that she has a mind of her own." He patted Aaron on the shoulder. "You're fine. Don't worry about it." He hesitated and said, "Hey, have you got plans for supper tonight?"

Aaron blinked, unsure how the conversation had turned from kissing women to eating supper. "No. I mean, I imagine the Koffmans will invite Maggie and me to stay and sup with them after we clean up, but…"

"I might be overstepping here," Mark said, still amused. "But maybe you ought to skip supper with Willa tonight. Let things cool down between you two."

Aaron groaned and began to pace. "I don't know how it happened. There's nothing between us," he insisted, trying to get the thought of her eyes meeting his just before he kissed her out of his head. It was like she had seen him, *really* seen him for who he was inside. No one had ever looked at him like that before.

Mark smiled. “Oh, sure, right. It was all my imagination that you two kept gawking at each other from across the kitchen this morning while we were all having coffee and doughnuts.”

Mark went on before Aaron could argue that he and Willa had been doing no such thing. “I’m serious about supper. Why don’t you and Maggie join Rosie and me.”

“I don’t know. I wouldn’t want to intrude,” Aaron managed.

“It wouldn’t be an intrusion. Rosie loves having guests for meals so she has someone else to talk to besides her little brother.”

Aaron hesitated. Right now he just wanted to get Maggie and return to the motel. He needed time to think. But Maggie would be so disappointed to return to that dismal room before it had even grown dark. Going to Mark and Rosie’s would be an adventure for her.

“Come on,” Mark urged. “It’ll be fun and Rosie’s a good cook. Not as good as the Koffman girls—well, better than Henry probably—” He chuckled and went on. “It’ll be fun, and maybe we can talk later if you want. Because right now—” He hesitated and then went on, his tone more solemn. “I think you could use a friend.”

Aaron nodded, acknowledging, at least to himself, that Mark was right. He could use a friend. "All right. We'll come for supper."

"Excellent." Mark patted his arm and walked away. "And we don't have to talk about Willa if you don't want to."

"I don't want to talk about her. I don't want to think about her," Aaron called after him. But, of course, that was a lie. All he wanted to do was think about how being in a room with her made him feel whole again.

Chapter Seven

Willa set down a case of assorted spices. Aaron had organized the area inside the apartment near the door, marking different categories in bold handwriting on white sheets of paper taped to the wall. Ordinarily, he would have brought any boxes delivered that morning upstairs, but he was on the phone trying to straighten out a banking error and the packages were blocking the downstairs hallway.

Aaron was a sore subject for her that morning. Her feelings were all over the place and it was his fault. At first, she'd been delighted by his kiss, then annoyed that he had acknowledged their unspoken feelings for each other. She'd been trying hard to ignore the attraction. Then, although they had agreed it wouldn't happen again, she'd hoped it would. But he'd made no further attempt to kiss her since they returned to work after the weekend. He seemed to be avoiding being in the same room with her.

Had he ruined their budding friendship with that one kiss? Had she ruined it by not pretending his advance was unwelcome?

Willa knew that Aaron understood they could never walk out together. He'd spent enough time with her family to see that neither she nor her sisters would marry a man outside their faith. So why had he kissed her? And why did she want him to do it again? Not that there was any chance of that happening, not with him dodging her like a rabbit with Elden's bulldog on its heels. He walked out every time she entered a room he occupied, using a weak excuse.

She exhaled in frustration as she slid the heavy box into place. The worst thing about the situation with Aaron was that she *missed* talking to him. She missed working beside him even when they weren't conversing. She didn't want to. But she did. And that vexed her, too.

Being upset with him was better than mooning over him, wasn't it? She wasn't used to not getting what she wanted. In the past, any boy she was attracted to showered her with attention, hanging on her every word. She didn't like the idea that she didn't have the same power over Aaron. But mostly, she just missed him.

"Last one!" Jane declared as she entered the room with a large cardboard box. She set it down with a groan. "I'll be glad when that addition is done so we don't have to carry this stuff up and down the stairs. Especially now that the downstairs storage room is the office."

Monday, Aaron and Eleanor had spent the morning trying to sort out receipts and count cash from the fundraiser on one end of the kitchen island while Jane and Millie baked banana bread and Annie chopped veggies to make five gallons of minestrone soup. Willa was taking a shift at the register out front at the time, but according to Jane, everyone was talking and laughing, as usual, and the commotion was making Eleanor crazy. Their big sister became rather cross, insisting she couldn't concentrate with all the noise. After Eleanor miscounted a stack of twenties for the third time, she slapped the countertop and announced that it was time she had an office. She and Aaron then spent the remainder of the day emptying the storage room and turning it into one. Any remaining supplies and inventory had been brought upstairs to the empty apartment, and while they were using a folding table and stools for furniture, two desks, two chairs and a filing cabinet would be delivered later in the week.

"What's in the box?" Willa asked Jane, pointing at the one she'd brought up.

"Jelly jars and lids." Jane walked farther into the one-bedroom apartment. "Millie wants to make more jam with the strawberries we froze this summer. She's going to put Christmas bows on them and add them to my gifts display." She set her hands on her hips and studied the large room. "This is such a cute place. I love how the kitchen and the parlor are all one living area." She turned to Willa. "I don't understand why Beth and Jack wanted to move."

"You know why." Willa lifted the last box into its proper place. "Because it was time they had their own house."

Jane sighed, looking at the empty apartment again. "Right. Especially with the baby on the way."

"Mmm-hmm," Willa agreed, shifting the boxes Jane had brought up. Her little sister wasn't one for details, but Aaron was.

Jane turned around slowly, her arms raised. "Maybe I can move in here when I marry," she said dreamily.

Willa chuckled. "When you marry? You're nineteen years old!"

"I'm nineteen out," Jane declared. It was a term their *mam* had always used meaning a person was six months or less until their next birthday.

Spotting a box Jane had put in the wrong place, Willa picked it up. "You know you have to have a betrothed to marry, right? Which means having a beau first."

"I know that!" Jane got a mischievous grin on her face. "I'm working on that."

"On which one?" Willa teased. "The betrothed or the beau?"

Jane became indignant. "The beau, if you must know, Miss Mind-Your-Own-Knitting."

Willa's eyes widened, suddenly realizing her sister was serious. "Jane Koffman! You better not let Eleanor hear that. That will be the end of you going to singings unchaperoned. You're too young for a beau."

"And why's that?" Jane crossed her arms. "You had one when you were eighteen. I think you had three or four that year!"

"I did not—"

"Willa? You up here?" came Aaron's deep voice from the bottom of the steps.

"Ya!" Willa answered, surprised he was looking for her.

Jane headed for the door as Aaron's steps sounded on the staircase. "I best get back to Millie's babies. They were asleep when I left them. Maggie's keeping an eye on them in case they wake, but one's bound to be awake soon. Then they'll both start fussing."

"We're not done with this conversation," Willa warned as her sister brushed by.

"I think we are," Jane whispered back.

And then she was gone and Aaron was standing there, filling the doorway with his big, handsome bulk. Willa returned her attention to a stack of boxes.

"I'm placing an order for supplies this morning so we can have them by Friday." He held a blue sticky note in his hand. "This says you need ten pounds of dark chocolate chips and ten of milk chocolate." He looked up. "Twenty pounds of chocolate chips. Did I read that right?"

Having him so close put her on edge and she began to straighten the boxes she'd just straightened to give her hands something to do. She desperately wanted things to return to how they'd been before he kissed her but she didn't know how to make that happen. "*Ya.* You read that correctly. Some recipes take one type of chocolate, some another and some both. We're selling Jane's frozen premade chocolate chip cookies as fast as she can make them. They're frozen dough, ready to go on a cookie sheet and be baked. You should be able to see that on the sales report for last week. Eleanor highlights items that are in high demand."

"That's fine," he said, sounding defensive. "I just wanted to make sure I don't place a wrong order."

She heard him turn to go and she spun to face

him. Without thinking, she blurted, “Aaron, are you avoiding me?”

He froze, his back to her. “What’s that?”

She approached him, lowering her voice. She hadn’t meant to have this conversation, but she didn’t want anyone to overhear them if they were going to. “I said…” She watched as he turned to face her. “Are you avoiding me?”

He didn’t make eye contact. “No, of course not.”

She stared at him and finally his gaze met hers.

He lowered his head with a sigh. “Willa, I—” He looked up. His brown eyes were kind and maybe a little sad. “I suppose I am.”

Emotion tightened her chest and her lower lip quivered. She knew it was wrong for many reasons but right now, it wouldn’t have taken much for her to fling herself into his arms. “Why?”

“You know why,” he said softly.

Their kiss, of course.

It was hard for her to believe that a little innocent peck could have become so problematic. A kiss that was one of the many she experienced over the years. Of course, Aaron’s kiss hadn’t been like the others. Because none of them had made her feel the way he had. The others had never made her feel anything at all. She couldn’t tell him that, though, could she? What would be the point?

Instead of mentioning the kiss, she said, "But I miss you. I miss talking to you." She smiled sadly, looking away because her emotions felt overwhelming. She was used to being in control of her feelings and she didn't like how this felt. "I miss working with you. Can't we just be friends? That's all I want," she fibbed.

He crossed his arms over his chest and was quiet for a long moment before he replied. "I'd like that. I'd like that because..." He sighed as if what he wanted to say was hard. "I could use some friends, Willa. Having dinner with Mark the other night made me see that. I had friends back in Paraguay, people I relied on. I miss them and I miss that...compass." He studied her. "You know what I mean?"

She relaxed in relief. He still wanted to be friends. This wasn't what either of them wanted, but it was doable. "I understand. A compass tells you which way to go. Our friends and family do the same for us. They guide us. Help us find our path. If they're good ones," she added. "Mark is a good man. He'd make a good friend," she continued as the tension eased between them. "Beth's Jack has nothing but positive things to say about him."

"He is a good guy," Aaron agreed. Then he hesitated as if to say something else.

She waited.

Aaron ran his fingers through his thick, dark hair, something she'd noticed he did when he was thinking. "He, uh… Mark invited me to go to church with him and Rosie tonight. It's supper and there's music afterward. Some folks playing instruments, singing. It's in the church hall and Maggie can come, too. He thought it might be a way for me to meet some people." He sounded uncertain.

She was surprised he'd brought up the subject considering how he told her he felt about the Mennonite Church. Any church. It was one of the conversations they'd had over lunch one day when no one was around. Before the kiss.

She smiled, pleased he felt he could talk to her about matters like this. "I think Mark's right. It *would* be a good place to make friends. I know some folks from Rosie and Mark's church. They're kind, thoughtful people. And fun." She tilted her head, watching him. "Are you thinking about going?"

He slid his hands into his back pockets. Today he was wearing another flannel shirt, this one a maroon plaid. It looked nice on him.

"I don't know," he said unhurriedly. "I don't

want to be rude. It was kind of him to invite me, but…"

She waited and when he didn't finish his thought, said, "But what, Aaron? Why wouldn't you go?"

He groaned. "It's still church, Willa. And… And I don't have a problem with others' beliefs, but like I told you the other day, I don't want any part of church. Not ever again." He shook his head adamantly. "Not after what happened to Ancke. Because if it weren't for the church, she'd still be alive. And Maggie would still have a mother. I'm convinced of that."

His words made her heart ache for him and she wanted to ask him what had happened to his wife and why he felt the church was responsible. She sensed this wasn't the time, though. Maybe at some point it might be, but this wasn't it. Instead, she said, "Mark's not asking you to join or even go to services, right?"

He nodded. "Right."

"So it's just supper with nice people. And music." She shrugged. "What harm can there be in a home-cooked meal and singing?" She could tell he was thinking about what she'd said and added, "And it would be a way for Maggie to meet other children. We love having her here with us, but she doesn't have anyone to play with. And with her not old enough to be in school yet…maybe she's lonely, too."

"I hadn't even thought of that. Before we came here, she had so many cousins her age. You're right. No harm in going for supper and some music. Maggie's never heard musical instruments. They weren't allowed in our church in Paraguay." He met her gaze. "Thanks, Willa. For talking me through this."

"Sure. It's what friends do for friends, right?"

"Right." He surprised her by reaching out his hand.

She accepted and he squeezed it warmly before letting go. It wasn't a handshake. It was different. More intimate.

As she watched him go down the stairs, she warned herself, *Don't fall in love with this man. You'll be left with nothing but a broken heart.*

The problem was she feared she was already halfway there.

Midmorning the Tuesday before Thanksgiving, Eleanor walked into the kitchen where Willa was making a big pot of hot chocolate to sell by the cup. They sold coffee year-round, but hot chocolate was only available through the holidays. It was a big seller, not just with children but adults, especially since it came with a free miniature candy cane to use as a stirrer.

"Aaron's still not here?" Eleanor asked, glancing at the wall clock.

Willa shook her head and slowly added the gallon of milk to the pot on the stove. "Still not here," she answered, keeping her tone even. A part of her was concerned, but another was annoyed. He was two hours late, which affected everyone there that morning.

Instead of running the cash register as planned for Annie, who was out sick, Eleanor had to meet with someone from the company to repair or replace one of the windows in the showroom that likely had a broken seal. That meant that Jane had to cancel plans with a friend to attend a quilting where they were finishing up a Christmas project so *she* could run the register. Willa had offered but Eleanor had a whole list of things to be done in the kitchen that couldn't wait.

Where is he, anyway? Willa wondered. Just because he'd practically taken over Eleanor's job in the store didn't mean he had a right to wander in whenever he felt like it.

"I'm surprised he hasn't called." Eleanor poured two cups of coffee from the percolator on the stove.

"I don't think he has a cell phone. He said he was getting one this coming weekend." Willa stirred the milk with a long wooden spoon.

Eleanor made a tsking sound. "But he could

have found a phone somewhere. It's not like him to be late. He's usually here early."

"Ya," Willa agreed, glancing at the clock. She'd been so busy that morning that she hadn't realized it was after nine. She wondered if he or Maggie were sick like Annie. Maybe he decided they should stay at the motel today. But if that was the case, wouldn't he have called? He knew what time they arrived at the store each morning and its number. He could have used the phone at the motel office.

She'd been disappointed when he hadn't arrived at his usual time. She'd hurried from the house to be the first one at the store, hoping to share a cup of coffee and some cranberry nut bread alone with him and Maggie before everyone else arrived. It was a routine they'd fallen into since their discussion about being friends. They'd both stuck to their word, trying to be just friends, but she'd been fighting her feelings for him and suspected he'd been doing the same.

"I wonder if I should call the motel," Eleanor said, adding sugar and cream to one of the cups. She had to be making it for Jane. They always teased their little sister about liking a little coffee in her sweetened cream. "I imagine they could connect me to his room."

"Ellie!" Jane called from the entrance to the

kitchen. "The workmen are here. They need to talk to you." She headed back to the storefront.

"Coming!" Eleanor grabbed the cups of coffee.

"Oh, I forgot." Jane was back again. "They also need to see the receipt for the window."

"Ach." Eleanor turned toward the hallway that led to her new office, then back to Jane in indecision. "I can't be in two places at once."

"I'll get the receipt." Willa turned off the flame beneath the pot of warming milk. "You talk to them and I'll bring it out."

"Danki," Eleanor said with relief. "It's in the new filing cabinet. I think the file says Building Receipts or something like that."

"I'll find it."

In the office, Willa opened the top drawer of the new filing cabinet. Only seeing files related to what they bought and sold, she closed the drawer. As she opened the second one, she heard the back door open and Maggie's voice. Relieved Aaron had shown up, she flipped through the files, marked in his handwriting. A moment later, she heard his footsteps in the hall. When he reached the doorway to the office, she spun around, intending to ask him why he hadn't bothered to let them know he was going to be late, but she never got the words out of her mouth.

Instead, she gasped. “Aaron, what happened?”

He smelled strongly of smoke and there was a streak of soot across his cheek.

He wiped his mouth with the back of his hand. “Sorry I’m late. I should have called, but—” He exhaled. “There was a fire at the motel this morning.”

Willa reacted without thinking, and ran the few steps between them to throw her arms around his neck. She felt him pull her against him and rested her head on his chest, feeling his heartbeat.

“Oh, Aaron,” she breathed, her voice muffled by his flannel shirt. “Thank the good Lord you’re all right!” His arms around her felt so right that it took her a second to relax her grip on his enough to look up into his eyes. “Maggie’s okay?” she breathed, her eyes teary.

“She’s okay,” he whispered, gazing down at her as he held her in the embrace. “No one was hurt at the motel, but the whole place has been shut down. We had to load our things into the car.”

“How awful,” Willa sputtered. “I’m so glad you and Maggie are all right. If I had lost you, I don’t know what—” She gulped, her heart pounding. “Aaron, I don’t want to be *just* friends.” The words burst from her mouth before she could stop herself.

"You don't?" he murmured.

She shook her head, afraid to speak her heart. Afraid to hear his response. "Do you?"

"I don't, but—"

She touched her finger to his mouth to silence him. "I don't care about the *but*s, and… and I don't think you do, either." She returned her hand to his shoulder. "I want to be yours and you to be mine."

He exhaled, still holding her. "Willa, we can't—"

"No one has to know," Willa interrupted. "That will give us some time to… I don't know. See if it's real," she whispered. "And if it is, we'll figure something out. I know we will."

He looked down at her, his face contorted in uncertainty, and Willa rested her head against his chest again, thinking she had never felt so safe anywhere before. She didn't care if it was crazy; she didn't care if there was no way this could end well. She loved him. It was as simple as that.

"Willa." He breathed her name, kissing her forehead. "I—"

"Aaron! Aaron," came Eleanor's voice, followed by running footsteps.

Willa was able to pull out of his arms and take a step back before her sister burst into the room.

* * *

"Oh, Aaron. I'm so glad you and Maggie are all right," Eleanor said, breathless. "Maggie told us what happened." She peered up at him. "I'm sorry you had to go through such a thing. You must have been so scared."

"It's okay, Eleanor." Aaron opened his arms wide, relieved she hadn't caught him and Willa in their embrace. His heart was pounding. Holding Willa had been such an amazing feeling that all he wanted to do was hold her again. He didn't care how it made no sense. Or how impossible the situation was. All he could think about was the feel of his arms around her and how much she wanted to be with him. He knew he could never be her beau. Not even in secret, but he didn't care. It was what he wanted most in the world right now. And she did, too. He saw it in her eyes, even now, when he glanced at her as he talked to her sister.

"We… We're fine," he managed, trying to shift his thoughts away from Willa. "The fire was at the other end of the building."

Eleanor looked him up and down. "But you smell like smoke. And you have soot on your face."

He wiped his cheek with the back of his hand. "When the smoke alarms went off, I put Maggie safely in the car and ran to see if anyone needed help. There's a man who lives—*lived*—on that end. Mr. Johnson. He's in a wheelchair. I wanted to make sure he got out safely. The fire was next to his room but I helped him get out. The paramedics took him to the hospital to check him over but they told me he is going to be fine."

"And the people in the room that caught on fire?" Willa asked. "Are they all right?"

He only met her gaze for a moment, then returned his attention to Eleanor. "No one was in the room. The firemen said there would be an investigation to find out what happened. They said it could have been a coffee pot left unattended or faulty wiring. They have experts to determine those things."

"And you were able to get all your things?" Eleanor asked.

"Yes, most of them. We had to wait until the police let me go back to our room to get our belongings. But we're fine."

"*Ya*, and that's what matters, doesn't it?" Eleanor asked. "The good Lord protected them, didn't he, Willa?"

"Ya," Willa agreed, sounding as if she were far in the distance even though she was standing close enough for him to touch her.

Aaron cleared his throat. "I need to change my shirt. Like you said, Eleanor, I smell like smoke. But I'll get to work after that and when I take a lunch break, I'll call around to see what motels have openings. We may have to go into Dover, but I'm sure I can find a place for us to rent a room."

"You don't want to stay with your aunt and uncle?" Eleanor asked, her broad brow furrowing.

"I can't impose like that," he said. "And they have a full house anyway with my cousin and his wife and four children staying there until their new house is ready in the spring." He held up his hand. "Let me go to the car and change my shirt and I'll get to work."

"You'll do no such thing," Eleanor harrumphed. "You're taking the day off. First, you're going to take a shower upstairs in the apartment." She pointed upward. "Then you're going to start moving in."

"What?" he asked, astonished. And touched at the same time.

"You heard me," Eleanor said, sounding as bossy as she did with her sisters. "You and Maggie are moving into the apartment upstairs. We'll put the supplies elsewhere. And I won't hear another word about it. I intended to give you a raise but if you're agreeable, you can take the apartment rent-free instead."

"No, Eleanor," he said adamantly. "I can't

accept free rent. Absolutely not. I won't take advantage of your kindness any more than I already have."

"This isn't taking advantage. If anything, I'm taking advantage of you, but fine," she declared. "The raise will be in your check at the end of the week. You can pay me what you were paying for the motel room."

"Eleanor, I can't—"

"I have to get back," she interrupted. "The workmen are waiting for me. You're moving in here and that's final. It's safer if someone keeps an eye on the store anyway."

He let his hands fall to his sides. "All right. Fine. We move in, but only temporarily," he cautioned. "And we will not be moving the storage boxes. The apartment is four times the size of the motel room we've been staying in. There's plenty of room."

Eleanor looked as if she was going to argue with him but then said, "Fair enough. Willa can find what you need at the house—sheets, towels and so forth. The bedroom has a double bed, but we have a twin bed for Maggie in our attic. I'll have Elden fetch it." She looked past him to Willa. "Can you get him whatever he needs? And don't listen to his nonsense about taking advantage of us."

"Oll recht," Willa said.

Aaron watched Eleanor go out the door and then reached out to Willa. “This is crazy,” he whispered.

She slid her hand into his, beaming. “It is,” she whispered back. “And I’ve never been happier in my life.”

Chapter Eight

When Thanksgiving Day dawned bright and crisp, Willa was bustling around the kitchen making a hot breakfast for her family. She'd always enjoyed the holiday because, unlike some of the stricter families in Honeycomb who fasted, the Koffmans celebrated with a big meal. They began and ended the day with family prayer. However, their day of thanks was also filled with good food and laughter, and Willa anticipated it would be even better this year.

She'd woken excited to share a bountiful meal with her family and her new beau who would join them. Unlike previous relationships, which she realized had often been about appearances, she didn't care that no one could know about Aaron and her. What mattered to them was that Aaron felt the same way about her as she did him. She didn't need anyone else to know. For the first time, she saw a relationship with a beau as being between *them* rather than something to be displayed for all to see and talk about. Now she didn't give a passing thought to having to keep their relationship a secret because she wouldn't allow that to ruin her happiness. For once she wasn't thinking about the future or making plans, wondering if this beau could be the one she would marry. She was enjoying her and Aaron's happiness, not thinking about anything beyond each day.

Aaron and Maggie arrived at eleven o'clock to help prepare the midday meal. At first, he had dragged his feet about coming, using the excuse that the family saw enough of him now that they were living in the apartment above the store. When Eleanor had dismissed that explanation as ridiculous, Aaron had said that Mark had mentioned possibly joining them for a Thanksgiving meal because he and his sister had no family in the area. Eleanor solved the problem by inviting Mark and Rosie, as well.

Willa and Aaron hadn't had an opportunity to speak alone since his arrival, but the presence of him and Maggie on such a special day made Willa happy. And several times, when no one was looking, they had managed to make eye contact, and each time, her heart had beat a little faster.

The meal was scheduled for one o'clock and by noon the kitchen was filled with bustling skirts and men trying to stay out of the women's way. After putting a huge pot of potatoes on the stove to boil, Willa carried the pail of peels out to the chicken house and dumped them in the fenced-in run. As she walked back to the house, enjoying the sunshine on her face, she spotted Aaron crossing the backyard, heading toward the garden, a basket in his hand. Curious about what he was doing, she cut across the grass toward him.

"Hey," she called when, deep in thought, he didn't see her.

He looked up and smiled, his face softening. He had the most gorgeous smile; he needed to show it more. "Hey, yourself," he replied.

She pointed at the shallow, rectangular basket they used for harvesting vegetables in his hand. Inside it was a pair of kitchen shears. "What are you doing?"

"Cutting rosemary for Jane. She said it was on the south side of the garden, near the holly bush." He nodded in the direction of a row of green. "I expect that's the rosemary. Not much else alive out here."

"*Ya*, it is. Eleanor planted plenty so we could sell it at the store. What's Maggie doing?" she asked.

"Elden dropped Millie off. I guess his uncle

isn't doing well so he and his mother are visiting him and the aunt for a while."

Willa nodded. Elden's father had died long ago and his uncle Gabriel had been like a father to him. Sadly, the older man had been diagnosed with cancer and was declining.

"So with Millie and the babies here, you can guess what Maggie's doing."

"She does love those babies," Willa agreed.

"She does. She loves them so much that she asked me if we could get one."

They both laughed and stopped to meet each other's gazes. Standing so close, she wished they could share more time alone than stolen moments in the store kitchen or office. It was hard working with him all day, every day, pretending they were just friends.

Willa glanced toward the house. Seeing no one outside or in the farmhouse windows, she grabbed his hand and pulled him behind the overgrown holly bush that would block anyone's view of them.

"What are you doing?" he asked, allowing himself to be led. He laughed. "What are we doing?"

"I want to talk for a few minutes without prying eyes," she told him, releasing his hand. What she didn't say was that she couldn't stop thinking about the single kiss they had shared and that she wanted another. "Did you go with Mark and Rosie to church again last night?"

"We did." He stood before her, looking awkward, the vegetable basket in one hand. He wore a knit cap and a puffy down vest over the blue flannel shirt she liked.

She set down the compost bucket. "How was it?"

He twisted his mouth one way and then the other. "It… It wasn't terrible."

She frowned, challenging him.

"What? It wasn't. And Maggie had a good time. After supper, we played board games—checkers, pachisi, Candy Land." He crossed his arms. "I'll have you know I'm the Candy Land champion of Poplar Branch Mennonite Church."

She drew back, raising an eyebrow. "Are you, now?"

He nodded. And then came that smile again and she felt warmth in the pit of her stomach. "You beat all the five-year-olds?" she asked.

"I did, as well as Mark's friend Fred, who I'll have you know is my age and has a daughter the same age as Maggie."

"Impressive," she teased. "Will there be a rematch next Wednesday night?"

He grimaced. "Sadly no. Next Wednesday after supper, the congregation will pack Christmas food baskets for needy folks." He nodded, glancing past her to the holly tree covered with its green prickly leaves and waxy red berries. "But Mark invited us to go with him and Rosie to church service on Sunday."

She heard hesitation in his voice and gentled her tone. "Would that be such a terrible thing?"

He ran his palm over his face. "I don't know. Probably not. Maybe." He exhaled loudly, his mind in obvious turmoil. "The people at Poplar Branch are very different than even the first Mennonite congregation I belonged to. Much less strict. Some women wear a *haube*, but not all of them. You know, the bit of fabric pinned to their hair."

She nodded. Rosie used to wear one, but no longer.

"They listen to music, many women wear pants, everyone drives a car, even on Sunday. They follow the teachings of the Bible, but they don't get caught up in Old Testament stuff like not wearing two types of fabric at the same time or not eating pork," he continued. "They seem to be very much about peace in the world. They do a lot of mission work in this country and others. I didn't know there was such a focus on that in the Mennonite Church. The one we belonged to was very insular."

He sounded animated when he spoke about Mark and Rosie's church and she wanted to encourage him to try a service. She understood why he thought he wanted no part of any church. It was no wonder. He believed his church in Paraguay was responsible for the death of his wife. And the congregation wanted to take Maggie from him. But she could tell he was beginning to see that whatever he was forced to be a part of in Paraguay was nothing like Poplar Branch. Still, she couldn't push him. He had to conclude that he needed a belief system again. In the meantime, she could only encourage him, so she shrugged. "You can think about it. If you don't go this Sunday, that doesn't mean you can never go. See how you feel."

He offered a thoughtful half smile. "You're right. You're absolutely right. I don't need to get myself all worked up about this. Mark hasn't put any pressure on me. He thinks…he thinks it would be good for me." He shrugged. "And maybe it would be. Who knows?"

She kept smiling as he spoke.

"I know I don't want my terrible experience to affect Maggie. I'm no fool. I understand that not all churches are bad. Not all religion is bad." He exhaled. "And I've been feeling much better in the last week. More hopeful. And maybe that has something to do with not only my feelings for you but because of how welcoming the Poplar Branch congregation has been." He looked down at her quizzically. "What are you smiling at?"

She took a step closer. "You." She tucked her hands behind her back and gazed at his handsome face. "I can smile at you, can't I?"

His grin broadened. "Only if I can smile at you."

She moved closer. "I want another kiss," she whispered boldly. "I can't stop thinking about it."

His brow furrowed. "I told you that was a mistake, Willa," he said gently. "That it wouldn't happen again."

"Not even if I want it to?"

He narrowed his gaze. "You're Amish. Aren't you supposed to save your kisses for your husband? I doubt your bishop would approve of you kissing a man behind a holly bush."

"I'm not baptized. I won't get in much trouble. I'd only get a good talking-to from my aunt, and I get those anyway." She took another step toward him, now close enough to feel his warmth and smell the fabric softener from his clothing.

His face softened and he reached out and drew his finger over a wisp of blond hair that had fallen from beneath her starched, white prayer *kapp*. "Want to know something?"

She nodded as she gazed into the depths of his dark brown eyes.

He continued to stroke her wisp of hair. "I've never kissed anyone but you and Ancke, and I didn't kiss her until after we were married."

Willa's eyes widened with surprise. "How could you have only kissed one woman before me? You said you married when you were twenty-two. By the time I was twenty-two, I'd kissed—"

He silenced her by pressing his finger to her lips. "Please don't tell me who or how many times," he said playfully. "Else I'll have a terrible urge to track them all down and—what does your sister say? Give them a piece of my mind?"

They both laughed and she felt an exciting tension cross between them. He put his arms around her and drew her close. "Willa, are we really doing this?" he whispered. He kissed the top of her head. "Because you know it can never go anywhere. You're an Amish woman, and I'm… I'm nothing. I'm not Amish. I'm not even Mennonite, technically, because I haven't rejoined the church. I'm an Englisher in the eyes of your family and your community. You can't marry me."

"I know," Willa managed, melting against him. He was so warm and solid. He wasn't embracing in any way different from what a family member or girlfriend would, but it felt significant. And so wonderfully different. "But I don't care. This is what I want."

"If I were a better man, I would end it now, but I... I can't..." he said. "I can't bring myself to do it."

She sighed, pressing her cheek to his puffy black vest. "Then we won't," she told him firmly.

They stood in the cool autumn breeze a moment longer, then he brushed his chin against her forehead. "I should get this rosemary and be on my way," he said. "Before I'm missed."

Willa made herself take a step back. "You're right. We best both get back to the house."

Aaron leaned down, took the garden shears, clipped several small branches and made them into a bouquet. "For you," he said.

Willa was touched. Boys had given her gifts before, but never anything so spontaneous. Or perfect. "Thank you." She took them. "I'll put them in a jar beside my bed and every night I'll think of you and again every morning."

She watched him retrieve the vegetable basket. "I'll wait until you've cut the rosemary and head to the house. I'll follow shortly. Everyone's so busy getting ready for dinner, no one will notice."

With a nod from Aaron, they parted and Willa clasped her Christmas bouquet of green holly peppered with bright red berries in her hand wishing he was Amish. Because if he were, she'd marry him today.

Aaron sat at the end of the kitchen table sipping coffee, listening to the Koffman family laugh about an incident many Thanksgivings ago involving people he didn't know. It didn't matter; it still made him smile. It was nice to sit in the warm kitchen and listen to the joy in their voices as he ate the last bite of pumpkin pie with freshly made cinnamon-and-maple whipped cream. It was his third piece of the day.

The midday meal had been the most amazing he'd ever had, even looking back to his days as a young Amish boy before his father left the order and became Mennonite. Besides a roasted turkey and duck, the Koffman sisters had prepared two kinds of potatoes, four vegetables including a spicy chowchow, biscuits, sausage stuffing, gravy, fresh apple cranberry sauce and so many desserts that he'd had pie and cake. After cleanup, Willa, her five sisters, their spouses, the new babies, her father, Rosie, Mark and Maggie had taken a walk together. It had been a family tradition since Felty and his wife purchased the farm. The stroll took them through fields and woods, past two ponds, zigzagging the three-hundred-acre property. After the exercise, they'd gathered in the parlor to play games and read; some even dozed off. And then leftovers had been pulled out, and he'd managed to eat an enormous sandwich made with turkey, cornbread stuffing, cranberry sauce and mayo, and the final piece of pie.

Aaron glanced at the clock. Beth and her husband, Jack, and his younger brother who lived with them were preparing to leave, as were Cora and Tobit. Henry and her husband and mother-in-law had already gone. It was time he and Maggie made their way down the long lane to the store and their cozy apartment. But he enjoyed the camaraderie so much that he hated ending the day. Maggie was going to throw a fit when he mentioned bedtime.

Millie's husband and mother-in-law had not made it back for dinner and were remaining at the uncle's house due to how ill the older man was. He'd been deemed terminal, but the family prayed that he would be with them for one more Christmas and were all gathering to lend the aunt support. Because Elden would not return until morning, Millie had decided to remain with her sisters overnight in case she needed help with their twins. Aaron couldn't imagine what it was like to manage two babies less than eight weeks old; he had been overwhelmed with only one. Millie had settled in a downstairs bedroom with her little ones, where Maggie and Willa were now.

Aaron glanced at the clock again and wondered if he could get Willa to walk outside. Since their secret meeting behind the holly bush, he'd longed to hold her again. Not that he could do it with Maggie at his side. Instead, he'd have to be content in remembering the warmth of her embrace and inhaling the sweet scent of her lavender shampoo. After Ancke's death, he was sure he would never love again, but then Willa came into his life, and now… Was it too much to hope there was some way through the chasm between them?

With a sigh, he rose, taking his mug and dessert dish with him. Of course, it was too much to hope for. And he was foolish to think otherwise. What he had told Willa earlier in the day had been true. If he were a better man, he would end things between them now before he hurt her. But he didn't have the strength. He needed Willa.

That thought was upsetting.

He took his dishes to the sink as Cora and Beth teased Jane about a twenty-year-old Amish boy who often stopped by the store on his way to work for a cup of coffee and a doughnut so he could talk to her.

Maggie skipped into the kitchen, Willa behind her.

"There you are, muffin." Aaron forced a smile he wasn't feeling, avoiding Willa's eyes. "Time for bed. Way past."

"Papa!" Maggie ran toward him. "Can I stay the night? Willa says I can if it's okay with you." She bounced up and down in her stocking feet. "Millie and Aggie and David are staying and Millie says—"

As his daughter went on excitedly, her voice seemed to fade. Aaron suddenly felt off-kilter, as if the kitchen floor had shifted beneath him. The first time his parents had kept Maggie from him, it had started innocently enough. He had worked later than usual one day and instead of carrying his daughter to their room in the motel-like building meant for newly married couples and families with fewer than three children in the compound, his mother had suggested he leave her to sleep with his younger sisters. The next night it happened again and then, on the third night, his parents met him at their door insisting it was better that she stay. It had taken him days to get her back and then, only after several visits from other congregants and their bishop who ruled the community with absolute authority.

Aaron covered his face with his hand. "No," he said. He slid his hand down. "No," he repeated, sharper this time. "You can't stay."

The room got quiet and he realized everyone was looking at him. Embarrassed, he took his daughter's hand to lead her out of the room. "I told you," he said, trying to keep any emotion from his voice, "it's time to go to bed. Your bed." He walked into the mudroom without looking at anyone else or saying goodbye.

Willa followed. "Aaron—"

"Willa, don't," he said again, sharper than he intended.

She went silent but remained where she was in the doorway. Behind her, he heard her family talking in hushed voices. Talking about him, no doubt.

Aaron grabbed their jackets off hooks on the wall. He squatted to help Maggie into her pink coat, trying not to look at her quivering lip. When her coat was zipped, he pointed to her shoes. She obediently dropped to the floor and put on the new sturdy leather booties he'd bought her the previous weekend. He still didn't make eye contact with Willa as he put on his coat, hat and boots.

He took Maggie's hand, heading for the door. "Thank you for the hospitality," he mumbled. "Tell everyone thank you and...and that I'm sorry—" His words caught in his throat and he couldn't finish his thought.

Willa grabbed a wool shawl and followed him

onto the porch. He wanted to tell her not to, but he couldn't find his voice. He was halfway to the steps when Willa spoke.

"Aaron, I'm so sorry. I shouldn't have sprung this on you like that."

He halted, Maggie's warm hand in his. His eyes stung and he fought to keep tears from welling up.

He heard her walk toward them. "You told me what happened. Why you're so cautious. I'm so sorry." She sounded as if she might cry, too. "I wasn't thinking."

Aaron felt Maggie's hand move in his and then she was holding his hand. "It's okay, Papa. I'll go home with you. I like our new home," she said cautiously.

She sounded scared, and that broke his heart.

"Oh, cupcake." He took a deep breath and squatted before her, gazing into her beautiful face. The funny thing was, while he saw his own eyes in hers and Ancke's golden hair, with it braided, he realized she resembled Willa, too. She resembled her so much that he could see why someone had recently mistaken her for Willa's daughter at the store. "Papa's so sorry for speaking like that to you. For using my meanie voice."

She blinked her long lashes. "It's okay, Papa."

"No it's not. We don't talk to each other with meanie voices, right?"

She beamed. "Right."

He gave one of her braids a playful tug. "Would you like to stay with Willa tonight and help Millie with the babies?"

Maggie nodded solemnly. "Millie might need me. She says David and Aggie like me. They like it when I sing 'Itsy Bitsy Spider' to them. She says it's soo-ving."

He laughed, turning his head to look away from her so she wouldn't see the tear that ran down his cheek. "Then I think you better stay."

"Yay!" She threw her little arms around him and squeezed him tight. Feeling her embrace, he knew he needed to be a better father, but he also knew he could do it.

He blew out a breath and wiped his eyes. Stood. "It's cold out. Run inside and I'll walk to the apartment, get your pajamas and toothbrush and bring them back." He lifted his gaze to meet Willa's. "If that's still all right with the Koffmans."

Willa's eyes were teary, too. "Of course."

Willa opened the door to the house for Maggie. When she turned to follow her, Aaron found his voice. "Willa, wait."

She looked back at him, then said to Maggie, "I'll be in in a minute. Go see if Millie needs anything." She closed the door behind her and turned to him.

Aaron gazed at her for a long moment. Standing in the golden porch light powered by solar panels, she was the most beautiful woman he had ever known. But it wasn't even her outward beauty he was attracted to. It was her heart. "I'm sorry about this, Willa. I don't know what happened in there."

"No need to apologize. I understand." She moved closer.

"But the way I spoke to Maggie. To you. In front of your family. It was wrong. I'm so embarrassed."

She smiled up at him. "You can't be embarrassed in front of them. They're family."

He started to disagree and then, realizing she was right, smiled. Because, while he didn't know how it had occurred, the Koffmans *were* family now. They had embraced him and Maggie with open arms and folded them into their lives.

"I don't know what happened in there," he said again. "I had a…a flashback I guess."

Her brow creased and he explained what the word meant. She nodded. "It's not been that long since you left that place, Aaron. You have to give yourself some grace." She took his hand and squeezed it. "You've been through a lot.

It's going to take time for you to see that Maggie's safe in Honeycomb, that you're safe," she added, still holding his hand.

He hung his head momentarily, taking in the truth of her words. He had to give himself the grace he would offer any other, and he had to heal himself. It was the only way he and Maggie could move forward beyond the pain they'd left in that extremist community. That realization made him think back to a conversation earlier in the day and a conclusion. "Mark and I talked tonight about church." He paused. "And I think… I think Maggie and I will go to the Mennonite services with him and Rosie on Sunday."

Her face lit up. "That's wonderful, Aaron."

"Don't get too excited, now. I'm going only to see what it's like," he warned. "It's not like I'm rejoining the church."

She tried to hide her enthusiasm but didn't succeed. "Of course."

"And…and while I know you can't go to services with me—"

"What are you talking about? I can go with you," she interrupted.

He drew back. "You can?"

She nodded. "This is visiting Sunday. We don't have church. We only have services every other Sunday, remember? I could go with you. My aunt might have something to say about it, but I don't care. I don't even think Eleanor cares what she thinks anymore."

He moved his hand so that he was now holding hers. "You'd do that? For me?"

She smiled. "Of course. Would it be okay if I bring Jane, too? She'd think it was such an adventure." She wrinkled her nose. "And it might give a better appearance."

He shrugged. "Sure."

"Then it's a date," she told him with a nod. Then she shook her head. "I can't believe I said that. It's *not* a date. You and I are *not* dating," she said firmly. "But do you think we could ride there with you in your car instead of hitching up the buggy?"

He shrugged. "Don't see why not."

They stood a moment longer, looking into each other's eyes, and then he let go of her hand. He feared they'd wind up in an embrace again if he didn't. "I better get Maggie's things." He went down the steps, looking over his shoulder. "Be right back."

Willa stood in the lamplight, her shawl wrapped tightly around her shoulders, smiling. "We'll be here waiting for you."

He grinned as he walked into the darkness, thinking he'd never heard sweeter words.

Chapter Nine

Willa groaned impatiently as she tried to re-pin her prayer *kapp*. The mirror in her bedroom was hardly big enough to see her face so she had to keep turning her head one way and another to get a better look. *You should be thankful you have a mirror at all*, she reminded herself. Some of the stricter households in Honeycomb still didn't allow mirrors for fear they would encourage vanity. The women of those homes had to put on their *kapps* using the reflection in window-glass or a dishpan of water.

Finally satisfied with her *kapp*, Willa went to her bed to fetch the sweater Eleanor had knitted for her the previous Christmas. Her sister had used a fine-gauge navy wool and created a cardigan Willa adored. It looked like what the Englishers wore, minus the buttons, which weren't permitted, not even in an Amish home like theirs. The sweater was perfect to wear over her blue dress to the Popular Branch Mennonite Church with Aaron and Maggie tonight. They were joining others to box donated canned goods to distribute to needy folks in the area. After the gathering, if it wasn't too late, Aaron wanted to drop some boxes off at the motel where many people affected by the motel fire were now residing.

Slipping into her sweater, she glanced out the window into the darkness. As she waited to see the headlights on Aaron's car come up their lane, she chewed her lower lip in nervous excitement. Originally, Jane was supposed to go with her to the Mennonite church hall, but she'd backed out at the last minute. A friend had come into the store that afternoon and invited her to go shopping and have a fast-food supper with her family. Willa had encouraged her to go, then felt a bit guilty. She genuinely enjoyed her sister's company, but not having Jane with them tonight meant she and Aaron could have conversations they couldn't in her sister's presence. It also meant they could hold hands in the car if they concealed it from Maggie in her booster seat behind them.

A knock sounded on Willa's open bedroom door and she turned to see Eleanor standing in the hallway.

"Ach." Willa pressed her hand to her forehead. "I'm sorry. I didn't get out the invita-

tions to the thank-you supper for everyone who helped with the fundraiser for Jon. But I promise we'll drop them off at the post office on our way home tonight."

"So you're still going to Poplar Branch Mennonite Church?" Eleanor asked, crossing her arms as if annoyed. "Even though Jane has flown the coop to eat pizza and walk the aisles of Target?"

"*Ya.* Of course, Ellie." Willa didn't like her sister's expression. "Why wouldn't I?"

Stepping into the room, Eleanor sighed dramatically. "I don't know. Because you're a young, single Amish woman, riding in a car after dark with an unmarried man?"

"He's not just some *unmarried man*," Willa scoffed, imitating her sister's tone. "It's Aaron! Aaron, who lives above our store. Aaron, who you trust to drop off our bank deposits!"

Eleanor said nothing so Willa went on. "I told Rosie I would come." She matched her sister's stance, feet apart, arms folded.

"Willa." Eleanor rubbed her forehead as if she had a headache brewing. "Do you think I don't see the two of you?"

Willa's heart skipped a beat as she tried to think what her sister could have seen. Yes, she and Aaron were spending a lot of time together at the store, and she'd gone to the Mennonite church with him Sunday, but they were rarely alone. Not with the store busy with the Christmas season in full swing. They were swamped with customers from the moment they unlocked the door until the closed sign went into the window. She had never gone to the apartment since he and Maggie moved up there, even though he insisted they continue using it as a storeroom through the holidays. Since Thanksgiving, she and Aaron had scarcely shared a private word, and the closest they'd come to holding hands was when she passed him a cloth napkin and his fingertips had brushed hers.

So why did Willa feel guilty? She met her big sister's gaze, hoping she couldn't read her face. She pursed her lips. "See what? Just say it."

"You and Aaron," Eleanor murmured. "Looking at each other the way you do." She pointed her finger. "I see the attraction between you. There's no other word to describe it. And soon others will see it, too. If they haven't already," she added. "You know that a match between you is forbidden. *He isn't Amish*."

Willa set her jaw in defiance but didn't speak because what was she going to say? Not telling Eleanor something was one thing, but to lie? She would never do that.

"*Ach*, Willa..." Eleanor sighed again and gentled her tone. "Have you thought any more about what we talked about a few weeks ago?" When Willa didn't respond, Eleanor pressed, "The matchmaker?"

Willa stiffened. *Not this again.* How could her sister have lived with her all these years and not know her better? "I told you," Willa said, trying to control her rising anger. "I don't need a matchmaker to find a husband. I won't have one," she added boldly.

Eleanor lowered her head, looking tired, which was no surprise. She'd spent the last three days running back and forth between the store and Jon Coblenz's place. He had several orders for furniture meant to be Christmas gifts and she was helping him with his children so he could make headway. "I'm worried about you," she said.

"Worried about me? Why?" Willa threw up her hand in exasperation. She was flustered and didn't want Aaron to see her like this when he arrived.

Eleanor hesitated, then said, "You're not going to like what I have to say, but..." She briefly looked down at their feet. "I'm concerned that this romance will turn out like all the others—leading nowhere. It's the only direction it can go because you're Amish and he's not. And then you're going to be disappointed. And hurt. Again."

Willa pressed her lips together, overwhelmed by too many emotions hitting her at once. She was hurt and wanted to defend herself. She wanted her sister to be happy that Aaron made her happy. Mostly she was angry with Eleanor for saying such a thing.

But what if her sister was right?

Willa had made many mistakes in her quest to find a suitable husband. For a brief time, she'd even considered Beth's Jack a potential husband—before he and her sister began dating. Every boy she walked out with or even had ice cream with, she imagined he might be *the one*.

Was she making another mistake? Was it time she started seeing the reality of her situation? Did she need to back away from Aaron before she got hurt again? Because she knew, deep down, that she could not marry him. And he knew it, too.

But how could she break things off? She was happier with Aaron than anyone she'd ever walked out with. She'd fretted that she might fall in love with him if she wasn't careful. What if it was too late?

"You should go," Eleanor said, intruding on Willa's thoughts.

"What?"

"You should go help out at the church." Eleanor pointed toward the window. "We can talk about this another day. After the holidays when things have calmed down around here."

Willa spotted the headlights of Aaron's car coming up the lane. She stared at Eleanor. She didn't know what to say. She wanted to be upset with her big sister, but how could she be? Ellie only wanted what was best for her. It was all she ever wanted for any of them. That was why she was sacrificing her own life, insisting she would never have a family or children. She was doing it for their family.

"I won't be out late," Willa said, heading for the hall. As she passed Eleanor, she rubbed her shoulder in a gesture that she hoped her sister would read to mean *I love you, even when you say things I don't want to hear.*

Aaron rested his hand on the steering wheel of his car as he hummed to a Christmas song on the radio, and Willa in the seat beside him sang along. Her rich, alto voice warmed him, setting him at ease in a way he wasn't sure he'd ever experienced. Was it Willa making him feel this way? Or was it escaping the religious community his father had forced him to become a part of? Or was this unfamiliar feeling that all would be well because he was attempting to reconnect with his spirituality? With God.

When Aaron had agreed to go with Mark

to events at Poplar Branch Mennonite Church like the Bible study he'd attended the previous night, he'd told himself it was to be polite. Then he assured himself that he went searching for friendship for him and Maggie. But he now realized he was less in charge of his life than he cared to admit. God was gently chipping away at his hardened heart. This was God's way of gently leading him back to the path he had wandered off in that horrible place in remote lands in Paraguay.

He eased to a stop at a red light and glanced at Willa. She was gazing out her window at twinkling Christmas lights lining the downtown street. Sitting there, he realized that his aunt, uncle, the Koffmans, Mark, and Rosie had all helped him along this path. But Willa had given him the courage to admit he was lost. She was the one who helped him realize that finding God and a community of like-minded people would bring him home. With her bright smile and honest, gentle encouragement, he had discovered the spark of a resurgence of his faith. He was finding moments of utter peace. Of course, he knew that a few church services, Bible studies and community service projects couldn't make up for all the time he'd lost, but Willa had given him a gift. She had given him hope.

That wasn't all she'd done. Not only had

Willa helped him, but she'd also been good for his sweet Maggie. He glanced at his daughter in the back, asleep in her car seat. When they arrived in Dover, she had been shy and quiet. And lost and scared. Like him, he realized. But Willa had shown Maggie love and kindness and how to have a good time. Having fun wasn't something that had been encouraged in the compound in Paraguay—not even with children. Willa helped Maggie see that she could make others happy and enjoy herself at the same time. Seeing Maggie beam when she could fetch a diaper or locate a pacifier for Millie and Elden's babies filled Aaron with joy. And love. Love not only for Maggie but also the young woman who had made it all possible.

A car horn sounded behind them, startling Aaron.

"Green light," Willa said, pointing to the traffic signal.

He pressed the gas pedal and eased through the intersection, turning off the main road toward home. *Home.* It was a word that made him smile. Paraguay had never felt like home, but Delaware did. He felt at home at the store, at Poplar Branch Mennonite and in the Koffman kitchen, where he and Maggie often ate. And it was all thanks to Willa.

As if sensing he was thinking about her, she

looked at him. "I had a good time this evening. Thank you," she said.

He tore his eyes from hers, making himself concentrate on the road. "No, thank you. I have no idea how I would have picked out new clothes for Maggie alone." After having supper at a pizza place, they went to a discount clothing store and purchased several dresses appropriate for Maggie. They weren't required to wear anything specific, but his daughter had begged for a pretty dress like the other girls wore to church every Sunday. The garb she had been required to wear before wouldn't have been warm enough for a Delaware winter, but he wouldn't have wanted her to wear them even if they had been. He had abandoned the ugly, coarse, poorly sewn sack-like dresses when he left that life behind. They had a new life now, and Maggie deserved every bit of joy he could give her.

"I think you would have been fine without me," Willa told him.

"I don't know. Can you imagine what she would have picked out on her own?" he teased, keeping his voice low to not wake his sleeping daughter. It felt good to be lighthearted.

Since his wife's death, Aaron had focused exclusively on Maggie and her welfare, but having a good job, a safe place to live and a new community was allowing him to relax. Knowing his daughter was safe and happy, he had started permitting himself to consider his own wants and needs. He didn't even feel guilty about it. He was enjoying this alone time with Willa. He'd been so busy at the store since moving into the apartment that he felt they had less time alone than before.

"You have a point." Willa laughed softly. "Had I not been here with you, you might have taken home that pink dress with the purple unicorns on the skirt and the sparkly plastic shoes with heels that lit up when she walked."

He laughed with her. "That's what I'm saying. I'm glad I had you with me. I don't know what's appropriate for a five-year-old girl to wear."

"You most certainly do." Willa waggled her finger at him. "You just don't know how to say no. You indulge Maggie too often."

He grinned. "Ancke used to say the same—" He caught himself before completing the sentence, alarmed that he had brought up his late wife's name.

How could he have been so foolish? He darted a glance in her direction. "I'm sorry, Willa. I didn't mean to mention Ancke. I'm not comparing you to her. Didn't mean to," he added, afraid he had ruined a wonderful evening by bringing up his dead wife. He didn't know much about women, but he'd seen enough jealousy in the community where he'd married that he knew better than to mention her to Willa.

She turned to him. "How could you say such a thing?"

He saw by the look on her face that she was serious and pulled into a small, empty parking lot of an independent Christian church. He couldn't give a serious conversation the necessary attention and drive simultaneously. He wanted to give Willa his full attention. "A man shouldn't talk about another woman to his—"

She surprised him by rolling her eyes as if he'd just said the silliest thing. "That's not what I meant," she said insistently. "I meant there's nothing wrong with talking about Ancke with me."

"There isn't?" he asked, puzzled.

She covered his hand resting on the console with hers. "No, Aaron. Of course not. Ancke was your wife. And she was Maggie's *mam*," she said softly. "I like hearing about her."

He drew back in surprise. "You do?"

"Of course I do." She squeezed his hand and his fingers found hers. "I like hearing about your life before you came here. I want to know everything about her."

"Why?" he asked, perplexed.

She smiled faintly and leaned closer. "Because she loved you and you loved her. She's a part of who you are, and I want to know everything there is to know about you, Aaron. I have many questions about Ancke, but I don't ask because I don't want to hurt you by bringing her up."

He sat back in the seat, unable to find the words to express his feelings. Willa's generosity of heart was overwhelming. Willa cared about his wife because he had loved her. Because she had been Maggie's mother and Willa loved Maggie. It was as simple as that and yet so profound. Willa had an immense heart.

When he found his voice, he said, "What do you want to know about Ancke? Ask me anything."

She pressed her lips together, meeting his gaze. By the security lamp at the corner of the parking lot, he could see that she was considering what she would say.

Willa leaned closer, creating intimacy in the confined area of the dark, warm car. "Her name. I've never heard it before. What does it mean?"

He smiled, remembering he had asked her the same thing on their wedding day. "I think she said it's Hebrew. It means 'God has favored me.' It's a form of Anna."

She smiled. "Such a beautiful name. And—" She lowered her gaze, then lifted it to meet his. "I know that you hold your bishop and that community responsible for her death, but why? What happened?"

He sighed, looking away.

"It's *oll recht*," she said quickly. "Aaron, you don't have to tell me."

"No. I want to. I just need a moment." He inhaled, then exhaled several times, then looked at her again. "Ancke had this spot on her arm that didn't look right before we married," he said, thinking back. "I thought someone should look at it, but…we didn't go to doctors." He exhaled. "We prayed. And after Maggie was born, it got worse. Bigger. I asked to take her to a doctor. I didn't know what it was but I knew it might be bad. I was denied permission and had no way to get her there even if I could steal one of the vehicles that belonged to the community."

He hung his head. Willa remained silent but slipped her hand into his.

"Then she started losing weight. She got this… this cough that wouldn't go away. I should have just taken her to a hospital in the middle of the night," he said when he found his voice. "I should have stolen a vehicle or hitchhiked. But Ancke didn't want to go. She kept saying she was fine. She wanted to wait until Maggie was older and it was safer to travel. Since we'd married, we'd secretly been saving money to leave the compound. She kept saying she could see a proper doctor once we arrived in the United States."

He gazed out the windshield into the darkness, seeing nothing but their reflection. "Ancke got sicker and soon she couldn't get out of bed. I begged to get help for her, but it was denied. They told me it was our fault she was sick. That we had sinned and—" He fell silent. "I won't tell you the terrible things the council and the bishop said. All I know is that Ancke died because she wasn't given access to the medical care she needed. She was so worried they would take Maggie from us that she didn't want me to do anything. My Ancke sacrificed her life for Maggie. For me," he finished, a tear running down his cheek. "It was skin cancer that went through her body. I figured that out later." He pulled his hand from hers to wipe the tear away.

"Aaron."

Embarrassed by his emotions, he couldn't meet her gaze.

"Aaron," she repeated. Then she gently touched his cheek and he turned to look at her.

Her eyes were filled with tears. "I'm sorry that this happened to you and Maggie. To Ancke. I'm so sorry."

Looking into her dark eyes, he was overcome with feelings for Willa. Telling her what he had told no one else about his life before coming to Delaware felt like leaping a chasm he'd feared he could never conquer.

Before he realized what words had formed in his head, he whispered, "I love you, Willa."

Willa heard the words, but it took a moment to register what he had said. Her heart melted because he meant it. She could hear it in his voice.

Then she got scared.

She thought of the conversation she'd had with Eleanor the other night and was afraid to tell him she loved him, too. Because what if she was making a mistake—like all the other mistakes? What if she wanted to say it back just because he said it? Others had told her they loved her. She'd fancied herself in love. Told boys she barely knew that she loved them and thought nothing of it.

But now she was afraid to say it because the words were precious to her. What if she didn't understand what it meant for a woman to love a man? Worse, what if there was no way to reconcile a love between them? Was there any need to exchange words that would never be fulfilled in marriage? And how could an Amish woman marry an Englisher? She couldn't, so why say it?

Aaron felt Willa's hesitation when the words came out of his mouth and he groaned. "I'm sorry. I shouldn't have said that."

"*Nay*, it's all right." Willa slipped her hand from his and sat back against the seat. "It's just… It's a lot to think about, Aaron."

"You're right." He hung his head. "I'm sorry."

"Don't be sorry. But let's not get ahead of ourselves," she said. "At some point, we'll need to have a serious talk. I know that. But not now. Not yet. After the holidays. For now, can we just enjoy being together?"

"And maybe a stolen kiss?" he said, trying to lighten the conversation. Willa was right. They shouldn't rush this, whatever it was. Especially because, right now, he couldn't fathom a way they could ever marry.

No, the smart thing for him was to enjoy his time with Willa, keep it simple and focus on the changes in his life and what they meant. Going to church and Bible study felt good but he had a lot to reconcile in his mind. After losing Ancke, he assumed he would never be again blessed by romantic love. He wasn't even sure that he deserved it. So many people went their entire lives without experiencing it once.

The thought chilled him and he started the car. "Let's get home before Eleanor sends your aunt out looking for you," he said, sounding far more lighthearted than he felt.

Chapter Ten

Willa sat at a card table in her sister Henry's parlor studying a two-thousand-piece puzzle of the Grand Canyon. Annie Lapp was on one side of her and their friend Liz on the other. The parlor was filled with card tables and folks moved from one station to the next, playing a different game or working on a puzzle. At a table behind her sat her brothers-in-law Chandler and Elden playing backgammon, and near them her *dat* and brother-in-law Jack played checkers.

"Five more minutes!" Jane announced from the corner of the room, deep into a game of Uno with several elderly women. "Then we switch!"

Willa smiled to herself. When Henry announced that she and her husband had planned a game night birthday party for her mother-in-law, Willa had questioned how well that would go over. Edee Gingerich had turned seventy-two that week. How many of Edee's friends would want to play board games with a houseful of twenty-some-year-olds? It turned out they loved the idea of celebrating with a younger crowd. Two widows from Seven Poplars who were currently playing Uno had hired an Englisher to bring them for the Saturday night party. One of the women, Dory Miller, told Willa over dinner that she didn't like her adult children keeping tabs on her and that she budgeted each month to hire a driver for social outings.

"Where did that puzzle piece get to?" Willa's friend Liz asked. She tapped the table. "It was right here. You just had it. The brown rock with the bit of green on the rounded corner."

Annie giggled. "It's a picture of the Grand Canyon, Liz. All the pieces are brown." She cut her eyes at Willa. "I think that's why Willa likes this one so much. Because it's hard."

Willa made a face. "I like it because I want to see the Grand Canyon someday." She admired the half-completed puzzle. "When I was in the second grade, we had a book about it. With pictures."

"And Willa snitched the book and got into a lot of trouble," Annie told Liz in a whisper.

Willa made a face. "I *borrowed* it."

"Her *mam* found it hidden under her mattress," Annie explained teasingly.

Willa pushed the puzzle piece Liz was looking for across the table to her. "I was going to return the book when I was done looking at it."

Someone walked into the parlor with a fussing baby and Liz groaned. "There he goes again. How long has it been this time? Ten minutes?" She rose and walked toward the door where her bashful husband stood holding the squirming infant.

Willa watched her friend take their son from her husband and felt a pang of jealousy. No, envy. She was happy Liz had found such a wonderful husband in Ezra and now had a beautiful baby boy. But Liz was Willa's age and had been married for two years. Willa had always told herself she had plenty of time before she moved to the next stage of life with a husband and children, but watching Liz and Ezra brought on an unfamiliar ache. It was bittersweet because she couldn't imagine anyone standing beside her but Aaron.

"Mind if I join?" a deep voice asked.

Willa looked up, startled to see Charlie Byler standing beside her. He was a friend of her brother-in-law Chandler's from down the street.

Annie giggled and covered her mouth.

"Um, sure. I doubt Liz is coming back," she told the handsome man who was around her age. "Jane will tell everyone to move to a different station soon, but I think she's winning at Uno so it may still be a few minutes."

Annie tapped the chair Liz had vacated. "Come on, Charlie. Help me find the piece to go right here." She pointed at a crop of rocks she was working on.

Charlie slid into the chair and gazed down at the table and then at Willa. "So… I hear things are going well at the store."

"Ya." Willa offered a smile and put a puzzle piece into place thinking she needed to find a new puzzle. She practically had this one memorized. "We're busy, all right."

"We can't keep our take-and-bake cookies in stock," Annie said.

Willa watched Aaron enter the room with an armful of wood for the fireplace. "*Ya*, especially Annie's white chocolate chip with macadamia nuts." Aaron made eye contact with her, then his gaze moved to Charlie and back to her. He raised an eyebrow. She pressed her lips together to keep from smiling.

"My *dat* had his doubts about your store," Charlie said. "What with your *dat* no longer being himself. My *vader* didn't know that girls could run a business. But I said if Willa had any part in it, it would be a success for sure."

Annie kicked Willa gently under the table, her eyes wide with mischief.

Willa flashed another quick smile at Charlie while stealing another glance at Aaron. Aaron tilted his head ever so gently in the direction he was going and then went out the door.

"I think I'll go see if Liz needs anything," Willa said. "Glad you could make it, Charlie." She rose off her stool and made her way out of the parlor.

Liz was in the hall, her back to Willa, bouncing little Davy on her shoulder.

"Need anything?" Willa asked, watching Aaron's back as he entered the kitchen.

Liz turned around. "*Ach, ya*, please. The baby's bag. Ezra can't find it. I'm wondering if he left it in the buggy." She shook her head. "He's a good man, but he'd lose his hands if he didn't carry them with him all the time."

Willa laughed. "Want me to fetch it?"

Liz grimaced. "If you don't mind. I'm afraid that if I send Ezra, he'll come back empty-handed whether it's in there or not."

Willa laughed and walked past her. "I'll look in the buggy, and if it's not there, I'll check around the house. I'll find it."

"Danki!" Liz called after her.

Willa walked into the kitchen where a group of women tidied up in preparation for the birthday cake. Her aunt caught her eye and she smiled sweetly, spotting Aaron, out of the corner of her eye, in the mudroom, which led outside.

"You should be helping your sister with dishes, not playing games in the parlor," Judy called.

Willa stopped near the end of the second table Chandler had put in the kitchen for the buffet line. Henry's meal choice had been as unconventional as the evening's entertainment. They'd had a make-your-own-taco night, which had delighted her mother-in-law, Edee, as much as the games. "I'm fetching Liz Fisher's diaper bag," she explained to her aunt, pointing toward the back door.

"And then you can put away all these dishes," Judy told her. "How do you expect to find a man if you don't practice your household skills?"

She shrugged, refusing to let her aunt spoil her good mood. "Wouldn't you say Henry did all right? She was never much for kitchen chores. I think Chandler does their dishes," she threw in, knowing she was only stirring the pot further.

Judy's long, angular face turned bright red. "But by the grace of God!"

"*Ya,* God provides, doesn't He?" Willa responded, making a beeline for the mudroom, the same direction Aaron had gone.

"Willa!" Maggie called when she spotted Willa. The little girl was seated on the kitchen floor rocking little David. Millie was pacing the kitchen with a colicky Aggie on her shoulder.

"Looks like you're doing a good job taking care of David," Willa said as she went by.

Maggie beamed.

In the mudroom, Willa grabbed her wool cloak from a hook and threw it over her shoulders. She imagined Aaron was on his way to the woodpile and hoped to catch him alone before she found the bag for Liz. Outside, however, she didn't see any sign of him. She glanced around the yard illuminated with solar lights as she descended the porch steps.

A cold wind blew out of the west, and to her delight, she saw a few snowflakes drifting downward as she crossed the frozen driveway to the line of buggies. They didn't often see snow this early in the year, but she'd heard that the *Farmers' Almanac* had predicted a record-cold winter with more snow than usual, which delighted her. She loved snow.

Willa spotted Liz and Ezra's black buggy amid a row of them and walked toward it, wondering where Aaron had gotten to. Had he gone to the barn on an errand for Henry or Chandler? Reaching Liz and Ezra's vehicle, she checked the back first. She was opening the swinging door when a hand touched her shoulder.

"Ah!" she cried, startled, and whipped around.

It was Aaron. "Sorry," he chuckled. "I didn't mean to scare you. I didn't want to call your name and get anyone's attention inside."

She pushed his hand away, laughing with him. "I wasn't scared. I just didn't expect you. Where did you come from?" She pushed him again, but he took her hand in his as she lowered it. "Don't do that," she added, her heart still beating too fast.

"Don't do what?" he teased.

"Sneak up on me!"

"Me? Willa, a man my size usually can't sneak up on anyone."

She held tightly to his hand. "I didn't see you when I came outside."

"Too busy thinking about that guy?" he asked, his tone still playful.

She squinted at him, moving closer. It was cold out and she felt his warmth even through her cloak. "What guy?"

He shrugged. "I don't know his name but I've seen him talking you up at the store's register. The one who showed up tonight after supper."

She still didn't know whom he was talking about. There were a lot of people in the house, and several had come and gone since her family arrived at four to help Henry with last-minute details. "I still don't know who you mean."

"The one who sat down at the puzzle table. I

saw him when I was stacking wood in the parlor. He was all eyes for you."

"He was not—" She suddenly drew back with a smile. "Are you jealous of Charlie Byler?"

"Of course not." He leaned close and she thought for a moment that he might kiss her.

She was disappointed when he didn't. He continued to insist they shouldn't kiss because it only made things more complicated, but they'd come close several times.

"All right," he admitted with a wry grin. "Maybe a little."

She rested her hand on his chest. He wore a plain black coat and a watch cap like the ones they sold for all the Amish men in the store. He looked more Amish than English in his dark, plain clothes and work boots. For a fleeting moment, she imagined him returning to the church of his childhood and marrying her.

But that wasn't going to happen. He'd made that clear even before they'd become romantically involved. He had told her weeks ago that he could never become Amish again, even though his aunt and uncle had hoped for that since he came to Honeycomb. It was foolish for her to wish for things that could never be, so she preferred not to think about their future at all. Englishers called it living in the moment and she was happy to do that for now.

"So *were* you following me?" Aaron asked. His brown eyes twinkled.

She smiled up at him. She liked this side of him and was glad he'd agreed to come tonight. He was rarely grumpy at the store anymore, but he had his business face on and didn't have time for this kind of innocent lightheartedness. Even though she didn't see as much of this side of him as she wanted to, it made her heart glad to know he was capable of playfulness after all he had been through.

"I was not following you," Willa told him. "I came out to look for Liz's diaper bag."

"That right?" He gave her exaggerated sad eyes. "Now I'm disappointed. I did everything I could to get you to follow me."

Glancing at the house, she spied movement on the back porch, grabbed his coat and pulled him behind Liz's buggy. Who left a birthday party before cake and coffee were served?

She gazed up at Aaron. They were standing close, facing each other. He had one hand on her hip. "*Oll recht.* I did follow you," she admitted.

"Yes!" he declared, but then he grew more serious. "Willa, you know we shouldn't be doing this."

"We're not doing anything wrong, Aaron." She moved close enough to rest her head on his shoulder. She wanted to tell him she loved him but was afraid to say it. Because if she did, the impossibility of their relationship might come crashing down on her and what would she do then?

He lowered his chin until it rested on her head, then turned his face so his cheek brushed her forehead. All the while, he was careful not to disturb her prayer *kapp*.

They stood in silence and she listened to his steady breathing. She faintly heard voices, the crunch of gravel under someone's feet, then the snort of a horse and buggy wheels going down the driveway. She closed her eyes, wishing they could stay like this forever.

Had he not gently taken her arms and stepped back, she might have never let go. "We should head back inside."

"Ya," she agreed, a bit overwhelmed by the strength of her feelings for this man who had lived a life so different from hers. "We should go." She walked around the buggy and opened the back to retrieve the diaper bag.

Aaron followed.

Sure enough, the bag was right where she'd hoped it might be. "You going to church with Mark and Annie tomorrow?"

"We are."

She smiled, shifting the bag onto her shoulder. "I'm glad." She looked up at him. "You seem better since you started going. Happier," she added.

He nodded. "I think maybe I am."

"See you Monday, then."

"See you Monday," he quietly called after her as she returned to the house.

Monday afternoon, Willa was excused from her task of making three dozen loaves of cranberry nut bread to go into Dover and buy twenty pounds of confectioner's sugar, a gallon of molasses and more sugar crystals to decorate Christmas cookies. According to a frustrated Aaron, there had been a mix-up with their order that had just arrived, and the missing items wouldn't be delivered for two days. The problem was that the store had several large orders for gingerbread and sugar cookies and that wouldn't leave them time enough to make them all by the Wednesday pickup.

Aaron was relieved Willa was willing to take the buggy into town because he'd dropped off his car the night before for repairs and Mark wouldn't be taking him to fetch it until the following day. To her delight, he caved and let Maggie go with her for her first buggy ride. Aaron allowing his daughter to go, knowing how hard it was for him to let her out of his sight, made Willa's heart swell. The fact that she was the one he trusted with Maggie for their first true separation since their arrival in Honeycomb made her love him even more.

As Willa eased the buggy off the road and into their lane, Maggie spotted the store and sat back hard on the bench seat. She crossed her arms and pouted. "I don't want to go to the store. I want to ride some more."

Willa eyed her, hiding a smile. "We already delayed our return, Maggie. Remember? I went all the way around the block so you could ride longer. Bert's ready to return to his stall and have some grain." She indicated the driving horse that twitched his ears at the sound of his name.

Maggie refused to look at Willa. "I want to go back to Byler's and get ice cream," she harrumphed, her arms still folded.

Willa glanced at the little girl in her pink coat and hat with its enormous pom-pom. She should have been annoyed that Maggie was being naughty, but she wasn't. Willa's *mam* had always said that she'd rather have a daughter with spirit than without, even when she misbehaved. It showed strength of character. Maggie was certainly showing strength of character these days. There seemed to be nothing left of the shy, quiet little girl Willa had first met. This Maggie was sweet, mischievous, helpful and annoying, and Willa loved every aspect of her personality. She loved her and her father.

That thought was sobering. Aaron hadn't pressed her lately about discussing what they would do about their impossible relationship, but she realized that putting it off wouldn't change the facts. It wasn't going to make the chasm between them any smaller. She couldn't marry outside her faith. It was that simple. She couldn't do that to her family. She loved them too much.

Maggie sniffed and Willa looked at her again. "Oh, cookie, this isn't something to cry about." She had picked up Aaron's habit of using words of endearment that centered on sweets.

"But I wanted to ride some more," Maggie said, wiping at a tear on her cheek.

"I know. But we can go somewhere another day. Maybe even tomorrow. Would you like that?"

Maggie smiled. "And maybe Papa could ride with us, too! I know he'd like it."

Willa covered her small hand with her own thinking how blessed she was that this child and her father had come into her life.

Half an hour later, Willa carried the last case of powdered sugar from the buggy into the kitchen. Maggie trailed behind carrying cookie decorations in each hand singing, "Joy to the world, the Lord has gum!"

Willa laughed but didn't correct her. She would leave that to her father. "Mmm, smells like someone's been baking," she said. "I imagine there's some cinnamon streusel somewhere around here for us to sample. Just to be sure Beth followed the recipe properly."

"And then maybe we can make cookies!" Maggie declared, bouncing on her tiptoes.

"Maybe we can," Willa agreed. As she helped Maggie out of her coat, Jane burst into the kitchen, the strings of her prayer *kapp* flying.

"Where have you been?" her younger sister demanded.

Willa handed Maggie her pink coat. "Byler's. Eleanor sent me for more—"

"Our aunt's been here!" Jane interrupted. "And she's given Eleanor quite a talking-to." Her eyes were wide with eagerness to tell Willa what happened. "I don't think I've ever seen Ellie so upset."

"Aunt Judy?" Willa handed Maggie her hat, pointing to be sure she tucked it into her sleeve. The day before, she said she'd left it at church because she forgot to keep it with her coat and they'd had to drive back to fetch it. "What were they talking about?"

"I don't know. I tried to listen at the office door, but Eleanor closed it and then—"

Eleanor's footsteps on the wood floor behind them startled them both.

"Willa!" Eleanor called. "I want to speak to you. Now."

Her tone was one of obvious displeasure and Willa met Jane's gaze. "Could you take her out front with you?" she whispered, indicating Maggie.

Jane nodded, wide-eyed. "Come on, Maggie. Let's see if Annie wants us to help at the register."

As Jane and Maggie left the kitchen, Eleanor appeared in the doorway to the hall.

"What's the matter, Ellie?" Willa asked, a terrible sinking feeling in the pit of her stomach.

"In the office," Eleanor answered stoically, then she turned and headed back down the hall, leaving Willa no choice but to follow.

Willa was barely through the office door when Eleanor said, "Close it." Her tone was sharp and a little scary. Eleanor got annoyed with her often, but Willa had never heard this tone of voice before.

Willa closed the door.

Eleanor pointed to a chair in front of her desk. "Sit."

Willa dropped into the chair.

Eleanor did not sit. "She saw you two."

"What?" Willa asked, confused. "Who saw what?"

Eleanor crossed her arms over her chest much like Maggie, but she was much angrier. "Judy saw you and Aaron at Henry and Chandler's the other night. Out by the buggies doing something unsuitable. She wouldn't say what."

"We were not doing anything *unsuitable*," Willa returned angrily. "We were talking."

"Willa, it has to end." Eleanor met Willa's gaze with steely eyes. "Today. Now. And there will be no discussion because I can't deal with anything more right now." She hesitated. "It has to stop, or I fear no decent man will marry you."

Chapter Eleven

Eleanor's words cut Willa deeply. Anger bubbled in her and rose upward. "Why would you say such a thing?" she demanded.

Her sister walked to her chair behind the desk and sat. "You know there are certain things expected of us, Willa." She looked up. "Our walk of faith blesses us with many gifts, but there are also expectations. Expectations for us as individuals and members of our church. You know very well that everyone in the community has eyes on our family because we're a household of women without male guidance. Our behavior must be above reproach. Unmarried women of the church are expected to behave in certain ways and you know that."

"I'm not even baptized," Willa retorted.

Eleanor pursed her lips. "But in this family, that has never mattered, has it? There is no *rumspringa* in Honeycomb. We're not free to run about sowing our oats before we settle down to a life devoted to *Gott*, family and community. We adhere to the rules our church and our district bishop set out, baptized or not."

Willa set her jaw stubbornly. "Sometimes the Koffman women bend the rules. *Mam* used to say that all the time."

"We do," Eleanor agreed. "Henry and her handywoman's business, our opening a store, you and Henry as young girls riding bareback through the field on our driving horses. But this is different and you know it."

"Because Judy tattled on me?"

"That's not fair," Eleanor chastised. "Our aunt came to me because she's concerned you're being led astray. She fears that your virtue is at risk with an Englisher. She's afraid I'm blind to what's happening between you two because I want Aaron to stay in Honeycomb and work for us." She pointed at Willa. "But I do see, *schweschter*, and it cannot continue."

"We haven't done anything wrong," Willa flared. "Aaron won't even kiss me."

Eleanor sighed. "Willa, you're not thinking clearly. You're smitten with Aaron. Like you've been smitten with so many boys."

I'm not smitten, Willa thought. *Aaron is not a boy, and I'm no longer a girl. I'm a woman in love. My sisters married the men they loved, why can't I?*

"Why do you do this to yourself?" Eleanor continued. "Why risk falling in love with someone outside your faith and suffer heartbreak unnecessarily? *Mam* used to say that if you never walk out with a man who isn't a potential suitor, you'll never fall in love with one you can't marry."

Willa wanted to tell her that it was already too late, but she remained silent. She was sick of her older sister ordering her around.

Eleanor fiddled with a pen on her desk. "I'm only saying this to save you unnecessary pain."

"Is that why?" Willa asked. And then before she thought better of it, she blurted, "Or is it because you're jealous? Because I've always been popular? Because boys have always flocked to me, and no one has ever been interested in you."

Eleanor blanched. "That's not it and you know it," she said when she found her voice. "I'm trying to protect you. Care for you. It's all I've ever wanted."

Willa rose from the chair without responding and yanked the office door open.

"Where are you going?" Eleanor rose behind the desk. "Don't leave like this. I..."

She strode down the hall refusing to listen to another word. In the kitchen, Beth set a tray of streusel on a cooling rack. "Do you know where Aaron is?" Willa asked.

"He took one of the cases of powdered sugar upstairs. We're out of counter space." Beth waved a hot mitt in her hand indicating a dozen cooling racks covered with pans of streusel and loaves of cranberry nut bread. "I imagine he'll be right down," Beth said.

But Willa was already on her way up the staircase. "Aaron," she called as she reached the top of the steps. "Are you up here?" She burst into the apartment.

She found him placing the case of sugar she'd just purchased on a stack of boxes. He smiled at the sight of her but then his face fell. "What's wrong? Has Maggie—"

"Maggie's fine," she interrupted. She closed the door behind her.

He stared at the door. "Willa, I don't know that we—"

"I love you," she declared, talking fast as she moved toward him. It was a relief to say the words that had been bouncing around in her head for days, maybe weeks. "I love you and I want to marry you. Today. Tomorrow. As soon as we can." She looked up at him. "I know we have to get a marriage license, but as soon as we get one, we can be married by a justice of the peace. And then I want to leave Honeycomb." She took both his hands. "Once we're wed, you, Maggie and I can go anywhere. We could go to

Arizona and live near the Grand Canyon. We can make a new life together."

He stared at her, his forehead lined with concern. "Willa, what's happened?"

"Just tell me you love me. Tell me you'll marry me, Aaron." Tears stung the backs of her eyelids as a sense of uneasiness came over her. Why wasn't he declaring his love for her? He'd already said it. How hard was it to say it again? "I'll be a good wife. I know I will. And a good mother to Maggie. I know I can never replace Ancke. I don't want to. But I'll love Maggie and I'll treat her as my own. In my heart, she'll be my daughter," she finished in a rush.

When he still didn't respond, Willa felt a flush of heat and she released his hands. What was wrong with him? Why wasn't he saying anything? She'd just told him she loved him and wanted to be with him for the rest of her life.

"I think we should sit down, Willa." His voice was hushed.

She stepped back, confused. Scared. "I don't want to sit down. I want to get a marriage license. You told me you love me and now I'm telling you I love you, too. Don't you want to marry me?"

He tried to take her hand, but she pulled it out of his reach. This was not the reaction she'd been expecting from him and she suddenly realized she might have made a terrible mistake. "Aaron," she breathed.

Not making eye contact, he ran his hand through his hair.

"Don't you want to marry me?" she repeated. That idea was beyond understanding. He had sounded so sincere when he told her he loved her. He hadn't been the first to say the words to her, but none of those boys had meant it. Had Aaron not meant it, either?

"Do you want to tell me what's happening?" he asked quietly.

"What's going on?" she demanded in disbelief. "I just told you that I love you. I didn't say it before because I wanted to be sure. But I'm sure now. I want to spend the rest of my life with you and Maggie as far away from here as possible."

He looked away. "Willa," he said softly. "You can't leave Honeycomb. You once told me you'd never leave your family. Doing something like this, running off and getting married without their blessing…" He gestured broadly with one hand. "It would mean not only separating yourself from them physically but emotionally, as well. And what about your church? Your family? You could be shunned."

"My family would never do that," she flung at him.

He was quiet for a moment, staring past her, then focused his eyes on her again. “Willa, I don’t want to leave Honeycomb. I have a home for the first time since I was a boy. I’ve found a new community. And I… I know it’s still early to say, but I think I’ve found the church where I belong. I think I’m finding my way back to God.” He took a breath. “And Maggie is happy here. She feels safe in Honeycomb.”

She stared up at him, bewildered. It hadn’t occurred to her that Aaron wouldn’t want to marry her. “You told me you loved me,” she whispered.

“I do love you.”

She shook her head slowly. “But not enough to marry me.”

“I didn’t say that.” He exhaled, noticeably frustrated with her. “Willa, we knew this would be complicated.” He moved toward her, reaching out. “Please tell me what happened. If you tell me what’s wrong, we can talk about it. I… I’m not saying marriage is impossible, but we have to think this through. We have to—”

“You told me you loved me and I believed you!” she cut in angrily. The tears she had held back sprang in her eyes and she gritted her teeth. *“I believed you.”* She met his gaze. “Forget I said any of this. I don’t ever want to see you again, Aaron." She pulled open the door and ran down the stairs.

"Willa, wait! Willa, please don't—"

Blinded by tears, she rushed down the steps and into the hall. She grabbed her cloak and bonnet off the wall and burst out the door into the cold afternoon. Thankfully, she'd not returned the horse and buggy to the barn and she climbed in. She had no idea where she was going, only that she couldn't stay there.

Aaron felt cemented to the floor in the apartment as he listened to Willa's footsteps recede. Then he heard the door to the outside slam. And then silence. He wiped his mouth with the back of his hand and found that he was trembling.

This was all his fault.

It had been wrong to allow his relationship with Willa to have gone this far. He should have known she'd be trouble the first time he met her. And not just because she was gorgeous. It had been how she took charge, expressing what she believed to be true, not caring what others thought. Not caring what *he* thought. It had been a refreshing experience after living years with women always at the beck and call of men.

Willa had reached out to him when he needed it the most. He hadn't realized at the time that he desperately needed someone to care about him and Maggie. But somehow she had sensed that he needed her friendship. And his motherless Maggie, she'd needed Willa, too. She had needed the entire Koffman family to show her how a family could be good and kind and walk God's true path.

Aaron never meant to fall in love with Willa. He'd never meant to fall in love with any woman again. It had just happened. He shook his head in anguish. What a fool he had been to tell her.

He squeezed his eyes shut. He had been blessed with such a gift when he met the Koffmans and what a mess he had made of things. He'd allowed his emotions to get the better of him, and now he feared that he might have risked his relationship with Willa and her family, too. The idea of losing them was nearly as heartbreaking as losing Willa. What if Eleanor fired him and told him to leave? What would he tell Maggie? It would break her little heart, too.

He walked out of the apartment and, treading lightly, down the stairs. He opened the back door to see that the horse and buggy Willa and Maggie had returned from town in was gone. He closed the door, not sure what to do. If he could just get Willa to listen to him, maybe together they could figure out how to make this all work. It would take time but surely—

The sound of papers rustling caught his attention and he walked down the hall to the office. The door was open and Eleanor sat at her desk.

She glanced up from what she was working on and tilted her head to look at him for the first time. He stared back, unsure why he was there or what he wanted to say.

Eleanor, who was around his age, wasn't the prettiest of the Koffman women, but she was attractive. Tall, slender and commanding, she had an angular face and the same dark brown eyes as Willa. He liked her and thought of her as a friend, which made the situation even harder because he didn't want to lose her friendship.

"Do you know, um, know where Willa went?" he asked when he found his voice.

"I heard the back door slam." She nodded. "I had a feeling that was Willa. She's the only one who slams doors around here."

He knew it was meant to be a joke, but neither of them smiled. He stood there feeling awkward. He didn't know what to say. He couldn't very well tell her what Willa had come to him about. Then Eleanor would know that he had fallen in love with her sister. After all Eleanor had done for him, he felt guilty for letting himself fall in love with Willa and then being foolish enough to tell her. Hadn't he known from the beginning that it would end with broken hearts and slamming doors?

"We…um, we had a disagreement, Willa and I," he explained, unsure what he would say if she asked what it had been about. He couldn't tell Eleanor. He couldn't betray Willa.

"I've been there. I don't envy you. I think we should let her be, Aaron. Give her some time to cool down. She can be impulsive. She acts on her emotions, not always thinking things through. But she always comes around." She smiled faintly at him.

"Should I go look for her?" He suspected she'd returned to the house, but what if she hadn't? He didn't have his car.

"I think we should leave her alone. Willa gets like this sometimes when people say things she doesn't want to hear. But once she calms down, she sees the truth. I think that's why she gets so angry. Because she knows we're right." She met his gaze. "We have to tell the truth to the people we care about. Even when it hurts."

Trying to get his emotions under control, Aaron shifted his gaze to a row of binders on a shelf behind her. They were bookkeeping records. While the Koffmans used electricity from solar panels and generators for the store, they did not use a computer. Eleanor's neat print recorded inventories, sales and cash flow. Until he'd come along and lightened her burden. "She said she never wanted to see me again," he heard himself say.

Eleanor sighed. "I'm sorry she said that, Aaron. She doesn't mean it. Willa… She gets infatuated. Then there's a disagreement and—" she shrugged "—then the infatuation ends and a few days later, it's as if there had never been a cross word."

The word *infatuation* caught him off guard. Did Eleanor know there was something between him and her sister? Had been. Why else would she have used the word *infatuation*? But he couldn't ask her.

"She probably just went for a buggy ride," Eleanor continued. "She'll be home later. She'll go to bed without supper, angry at all of us, and by morning, she'll be over it and back to herself. You'll see. She'll come to work as if your disagreement never took place."

He nodded and turned to go. "Will you tell her I'm sorry for me?"

"I will," Eleanor answered.

She surprised him then by calling his name and he stopped but kept his back to her. He didn't want her to see the tears in his eyes.

"Thank you," Eleanor said. "Not just for all your work here, but the joy you've brought. Maggie is a delight and you're just the man we needed around here. You'll always be welcome at the Koffman table. Always," she repeated.

"Thank you," he murmured as he went out the door, closing it softly behind him.

Willa drove the buggy aimlessly along the country roads she had known since childhood. She drove past the one-room schoolhouse she and her sisters had attended. She went by Mast's Orchard where they sold apples, and baked goods from the Koffman store. She took the long way to her sister Henry's in Rose Valley, but she didn't stop in. She didn't want to talk to anyone. As she drove, she cried and thought of everything she should have said to Eleanor. To Aaron. And then she cried some more.

She couldn't believe she had found true love and he didn't love her back. At least not enough to marry her. The conversation she'd had with Eleanor just before Aaron and Maggie had come into their lives came back to her. Ellie had said that while Willa had dated many boys, none wanted to take her for his wife. And she was right. No one wanted to wed her. Not even the man she loved. Eleanor suggested that Willa was unable to find a husband on her own, would *be* unable. And that was turning out to be true.

So if Willa did want a husband and family, she'd have to do something about it.

By the time Willa reached home, the store was dark except for a flicker of light in one of the windows in the second story. Aaron's apartment. She looked away and followed the long lane to the barn. She was thankful no one came out to help her remove the harness, brush Bert down and give him his well-deserved portion of oats. Moving through the familiar tasks gave her time to let go of her anger, at least for the moment, and devise a plan. Eleanor and Jane were cleaning up the supper dishes when she entered the kitchen. Their father sat in his chair at the head of the kitchen table slurping a cup of coffee and finishing off a piece of sweet potato pie. The room smelled of fresh pine boughs, wood smoke, cinnamon and nutmeg.

"There you are," her *dat* greeted. "All my chicks are here now and I can go to bed."

Willa kissed her father's weathered cheek, pleased that he was doing well so late in the day. Sometimes he woke up in the morning almost seeming like himself again, but as the day progressed, he lost his ability to do simple tasks. Speaking became hard because he couldn't find the right words, and by nightfall, he didn't recognize his daughters at the supper table.

"I see you had pie for supper," Willa teased as she removed her cloak and wool bonnet.

Her father laughed and took another forkful. "Nobody around here lets me eat pie for supper," he told her between bites. "I had to eat stew first and plenty of it."

Jane took Willa's outer garments from her. "We saved you some. Beef stew, biscuits and pie."

"I'm not hungry," Willa said, suddenly feeling exhausted. "I'm going to bed." As she passed Eleanor, she made eye contact. She wasn't angry with Eleanor anymore. It was her sister's job as the head of the household to tell her the truth, even when the truth was unpleasant. "I'm not scheduled to work the register tomorrow. I'd like to deliver the invitations by hand."

They were going to host a luncheon on Christmas Eve for all the volunteers who had made the fundraiser for Jon and his family so successful. Because the store would be closed from December 23 until the new year, they decided to hold it there because if they moved the shelving, there would be room to set up plenty of tables to host the sit-down meal.

Eleanor looked at Willa, concern in her brown eyes.

"I'd like to do that instead of work tomorrow," Willa pressed. "If you can do without me in the kitchen."

"Of course." Eleanor dried her hands with a

kitchen towel. "I think hand-delivering them would be a nice touch."

"See you in the morning," Willa said as she left the kitchen. *And tomorrow my new life will begin.*

Chapter Twelve

It was late afternoon when Willa drove into Sara Yoder's barnyard in the Amish community of Seven Poplars. She'd purposely made it her last stop of the day, even though it would take her an hour to get home. She'd decided to drop the final invitation to the Christmas Eve luncheon at the widow's to give herself plenty of time to think over her decision.

It had been nice to have time to herself without Eleanor or her other sisters giving her unsolicited advice. The hours alone gave her time to think and pray. At each stop, she visited with the invitation recipient for a few minutes, then excused herself, explaining that she had more invitations to deliver because so many folks had been willing to give their time to help the Coblenz family. Midday she'd stopped at Byler's Store and bought herself a sandwich, a bag of chips and a grape soda and sat in the buggy to enjoy it. As she ate, she thought of the day she and Aaron had done the same, only they'd eaten in his car with Maggie chattering in the back seat.

She'd been pretty good about not dwelling on Aaron but couldn't stop thinking about Maggie. She had hoped the little girl would be her daughter one day, which wasn't going to happen. Aaron didn't want to marry her and she had to get past that hurt and anger. She had to move on with her life, so she was seeing Sara.

A brown-and-white Corgi barked excitedly as Willa stepped down from the buggy in the barnyard. Once she tied Bert to the hitching post, the pup escorted her to the wide porch of the neat white house. By the time she made it up the steps, Sara Yoder stood in the doorway, her smile broad, her dark brown eyes bright.

"Well, if it isn't Willa Koffman," the woman greeted. *"Welkom."*

Willa guessed the matchmaker was in her fifties or early sixties. Sara was about Willa's height, but the resemblance ended there. While Willa was a blond, Sara's hair was walnut brown and so curly as to be almost wrinkled...what she could see under her black prayer *kapp*. Her skin was the color of her morning coffee with extra dollops of heavy cream. Sara was a puzzle: not black or white but an exotic mixture. She was unusual because most Amish hailing originally from Wisconsin were as pale as winter cream.

"I've come to deliver an invitation for a Christmas luncheon. A thank-you from our family and Jon Coblenz for your help with the fundraiser." Willa held up the envelope.

Jane and their *dat* had made them all by hand using old Christmas cards. Her sister had handwritten the details on new cardstock and their father had cut out pictures from the cards and glued them on the front. Jane had let him sprinkle some white glitter for snow, which had delighted him and kept him busy for hours.

"The details are inside," Willa explained, her mood lifting with the sight of Sara so pleased by her visit. "It's the twenty-fourth."

Sara pressed her hands together in obvious delight. "I love a Christmas luncheon!" She waved her in. "Come, come, it's a cold day. You must have tea before you're on your way again."

Willa followed her into the house, a single story that had once been an Englisher's home. Over the years, Sara had added a large kitchen and raised the roof for dormitory-style bedrooms for her guests. As a matchmaker, Sara not only arranged marriages locally but also brought single men and women from other states to stay with her while she found them spouses. The single women slept upstairs while the men stayed in an old barn converted into another dormitory.

"You picked a good time to stop by. I have the place all to myself for once," Sara said, leading Willa into a mudroom where they dispensed of her bonnet and cloak. "I have a houseful of women and a barn full of men for the holidays, but they're all out for a few hours. The women have gone to Fifers to get apples to make pies and the men have been sent to do some repairs on a friend's barn."

They walked into a huge kitchen where there were two identical dining tables that looked big enough to easily seat twelve at each one. Along one wall were a commercial-sized stove and a refrigerator the size of the one in the kitchen in the Koffman store, both run on propane. And there were not one but two deep farmhouse sinks. Cabinets painted a pretty dark blue hung above the appliances and lined one wall. A long island, with stools on one side, divided the working area from the eating.

"This is beautiful," Willa remarked, inhaling the sweet smell of freshly baked gingerbread. She'd been to Sara's many times over the years for events for singles, but never in the house. Sara hosted most of her singings and suppers in a barn renovated for such occasions.

"*Danki.* Can I get you some tea and a slice

of my gingerbread?" Sara asked, but she was already bustling around, setting a water kettle on the stove. "Leave the invitation there on the counter and sit." She waved at a small table near a bay of floor-to-ceiling windows on the far side of the room. There were two placemats and a small potted poinsettia on it.

Willa studied the table as she took a chair, trying to figure out why it was there. She'd never seen a table so small in an Amish kitchen. It almost looked like it belonged in a restaurant. "This is nice," she observed, looking out the window at a row of pine trees interspersed with holly bushes with red, waxy berries. The tree made her think of the holly berry bouquet Aaron had given her only a few weeks ago and she had to take a deep breath.

It seemed like a lifetime ago that they had laughed and flirted behind that holly bush on Thanksgiving Day.

Willa pressed her lips together, misty-eyed. She took another deep breath, reminding herself that all would be well. She had never swayed from believing that *Gott* had a husband for her. It had just taken her until now to realize that she had to give up control and let Him bring her intended spouse to her.

"This table, it's…unusual," Willa remarked.

"It's for courting," Sara explained as she gathered plates, forks and teacups with saucers for a tray.

Willa raised her eyebrows in surprise.

"I have them all over the house and a few in the yard when the weather is better. Once I've made a match, I like young folks to talk together without distraction. I'm very good at what I do, but it's not until they spend time together sharing their thoughts that we know for sure." Sara flashed a smile, showing even, white teeth. "My courting tables offer privacy without impropriety. Some of my girls come from very strict households," she went on as she carried the tray to the table. "Last month I had a shy little thing come with her parents from Ohio. They hired a driver and escorted her all the way here and then three weeks later came back for her once I'd found her a husband."

"How old was she that they didn't trust her to travel alone or with a sister or friend?" Willa asked, accepting a green cloth napkin with a sprig of holly embroidered on it.

"Thirty-four," Sara answered with a straight face. Then she laughed. "I know, old enough for an eight-hour drive on her own." She shrugged and then motioned to a plate of gingerbread. "Help yourself, I'll just get the tea."

Willa hadn't thought she was hungry, but her mouth watered when she inhaled the strong scent of molasses, clove and cinnamon. She set a large square on her plate and one on Sara's.

The older woman returned with a dark green pottery teapot, a sugar bowl and two small matching pitchers on the tray. "My Christmas tea set," she explained, removing one item at a time to place them on the small table. "A gift from thankful parents. The napkins, too."

Sara set the tray on one of the big kitchen tables and sat across from Willa. "I hope tea is *oll recht*. I'm a tea drinker. But I have coffee if you prefer. I don't care for it, but I've learned to make a good cup, or so I'm told. The young men who pass through here arrive thinking that coffee is the only appropriate hot drink for a man." She winked. "Soon enough they learn how satisfying tea can be, especially in the presence of a single woman."

Willa watched as Sara poured milk from one of the pitchers into her cup and then added two spoons of sugar. Then a third.

"I like to heat the milk and put it in my cup first," Sara explained. "Do you like milk in your tea?"

"Just sugar," Willa said. "What's in the other pitcher?"

Sara smiled slyly. "Lemon curd for the gingerbread."

Willa grinned. She loved lemon curd. Jane

had a recipe for tiny shortbread sandwich cookies filled with lemon curd. She only made them for the family for Christmas and never sold them at the store because they were labor-intensive. It was a special treat everyone in the house looked forward to each year.

"Try it!" Sara encouraged as she poured black tea into Willa's cup.

Willa poured a heavy dollop of the warm curd onto her slice of gingerbread.

"Oh, goodness, you need more than that," Sara encouraged.

Willa added some more and watched it slide over the sides of the dark, dense cake.

"A bit of lemon in every bite, that's what I like." Covering her slice of gingerbread in the lemon curd, Sara used her fork to take a big bite.

Willa did the same. "*Ach!* This is so good, Sara," she said as she swallowed. "My sister Jane would love to have this recipe. I think she'd agree it's better than hers."

"Certainly. I'll write it down before you go." Sara patted her mouth with her napkin and reached for her teacup. "Now. Tell me why you're *really* here," she said, her dark eyes gazing over the edge of the rim.

Sara's directness startled Willa. Was it that obvious on her face that she had an underlying reason for her visit? "I… I did come to bring you the invitation. I delivered them all over Kent County today. Everyone who helped with the fundraiser with donations or their time got one."

Sara slurped her tea. "You could have put a stamp on it."

Willa stirred her tea, stalling for time. Now that the moment was upon her, she didn't know if she could say aloud what she wanted from Sara. But she had to say it. She wanted a husband, and as Eleanor had pointed out, she had proved time and time again that she couldn't find one on her own.

Willa took a sip of the tea. It was strong, bitter and sweet all at the same time and as its warmth spread down her throat, she found the nerve to say, "A husband. That's what I want. What I need. Could you find me a husband?"

Sara sat back in her chair, narrowing her gaze. She stared so long at her that Willa began to feel uncomfortable.

"Is this what you want, Willa, or is this Eleanor speaking?" She went on without waiting for a reply. "Because your sister and I have talked about you before. I know she wanted you to come to me, but I'm not in the business of making matches for folks not wanting them."

Willa gripped her cup with both hands, choosing her words carefully. "It's true that

Ellie has brought up hiring you to me before, but…" She took a deep breath. "This is what I want. I'm certain of it." She nodded with conviction. "I want you to choose a husband for me, Sara. I've walked out with more boys than I can count. I've tried to find a husband for years and failed. I want a match and I want one as soon as possible. By Christmas," she added hastily.

Sara arched a dark brow. "I see." She leaned back in her chair. "I'll have to ask you some questions, but there might be a few possibilities here. May I ask you why you're suddenly in such a hurry?"

Willa smoothed a bit of lemon curd across her gingerbread with her fork, avoiding eye contact. "It's just time, Sara. Most of my sisters are married. Millie has two babies, and Beth is expecting— Did you know that Millie and I are twins? She's been married for ages, and—" She pushed a forkful of gingerbread into her mouth and chewed, then swallowed before she spoke again. "I'm ready. I don't want to ride home from singings with boys anymore, wondering if this might finally be the one. I want you to choose a man for me. I know how successful your matches are. Men and women come from all over the country, even from Canada, to have you find them a spouse."

Sara studied her intently. "And you're telling

me that you'll accept the man I offer, no argument, should I think I've found a good match?"

Willa swallowed. "I will. And I don't want to go on dates or have a long courtship. I just want you to find me a husband. Because… I trust you," she said. *I trust you more than myself.*

Aaron drove the ax deep into the log, and it split with a satisfying crack. He'd been at it since three, and the woodpile behind the store was growing steadily; there would be plenty for the woodstove that kept the showroom cozy. He'd forgotten how much effort splitting wood took as there had always been others to do it in Paraguay. Woodcutting kept a man's body in good shape and prevented him from thinking too much about things that troubled him. At least, he'd hoped it might.

It wasn't. He couldn't help going over the last conversation he and Willa had shared two days after she told him she never wanted to see him again. She'd calmly apologized for her rash words and behavior and promised that even though they no longer had a relationship, nothing had changed between her and Maggie. He had tried to talk to her. He had wanted to tell her that he did love her and that his heart had soared when she told him she felt the same way. When she'd come to the apartment, she'd taken him by surprise. He wanted to tell her that he needed some time to figure things out, for them to do so together, but she hadn't let him get a word in edgewise.

Aaron had tried multiple times to talk to Willa again over the next few days, but she'd refused and purposely avoided being alone so he couldn't approach her. And now he feared that he'd lost her.

He kept trying to tell himself that maybe it was all for the best, but he didn't feel that way. Even though he saw Willa on and off all day, it wasn't the same as it had been and he missed her. He missed the man he was when he was with her.

"Aaron!"

He sank the ax's blade into the chopping block and saw Mark walking across the frozen ground toward him.

"I guess you didn't hear me calling? It's quitting time, buddy." He looked at the watch. "Past time."

"Sorry. Lost in my thoughts, I guess." He stepped away from the woodpile, pulled off his leather work gloves and inhaled deeply. He was tired from the exertion. Hopefully, he'd finally sleep well instead of tossing and turning, wishing things had turned out differently with Willa.

Mark shoved his hands into his pockets and

hunched his shoulders over. "You want to come over for supper tonight?" He tilted his head in the direction of his truck. "Once I drop off the guys, I'm headed home. Rosie's making meat-loaf and mashed potatoes. Something called a Noel log for dessert. She says she's practicing making it for the Christmas Eve brunch."

Aaron exhaled and reached for his down vest. He'd shed it when he'd gotten overheated but now that he was standing still, he realized the temperature had dropped. "I don't know. We've been over for supper twice this week." He glanced at his friend. "You really want us again?"

"I was thinking maybe just you. Maggie's inside chattering about having a sleepover with Willa. Something about learning to darn socks after supper?" He shrugged. "I figured you could use a night off from dad duties. Hang out with me and Rosie. We could play a game or something after supper."

Aaron hesitated. He wouldn't tell Maggie she couldn't sleep over with the Koffmans. He couldn't do that to her. If his daughter had noticed that things were different between him and Willa, she hadn't said. And Willa was right, just because they were no longer whatever they had been before, that didn't have to affect her relationship with Maggie. That would break Maggie's heart.

However, he was concerned about going to Mark and Rosie's again, especially without Maggie. Mark hadn't come out and said so, but Aaron got the idea that he was trying to play matchmaker, thinking that his sister might make a good wife for Aaron.

Two days ago, in a weak moment, he'd told Mark about his brief romance with Willa and how it had ended. Mark had listened, and sensing that Aaron didn't want to discuss it, he hadn't brought it up again. Aaron got the impression Mark knew more than he let on. He expected it was the same with the Koffman girls. None of the sisters said anything, but there were lots of conversations between the women that ended abruptly whenever he walked into a room. Eleanor was acting strange, too. Looking back, he suspected she'd had an idea what was going on that day when Willa had ended things with him. But he hadn't brought it up and neither had Eleanor. What was the point?

Aaron glanced up at Mark. "Thanks for the invitation, but I think I'll turn in early tonight." He grabbed the ax. "With Christmas in two weeks, the store has been crazy busy. I'm going to get up early and try to tackle some paperwork before we open for the day. It's always easier to run numbers when there aren't half a dozen people asking you questions."

"On a Saturday?" Mark asked. "Do you ever rest?"

Aaron dug deep and managed a smile. "That's what Sundays are for."

Mark nodded but made no move toward his truck. "You know when you told me about what happened with Willa, I got the idea you didn't want my opinion on the matter, but… Are you sure it's over?" He shrugged. "You know Rosie and I were once Amish. More young folks are becoming Mennonites. I understand why you wouldn't consider becoming Amish again, but did you and Willa ever talk about…you know, her converting?"

Aaron opened his arms wide, sadness washing over him. "We never got that far. And now she barely speaks to me." He hesitated. "It's over, Mark."

And the sooner he accepted it, the better off he'd be.

Chapter Thirteen

Willa heard the cellar door open and Eleanor called her name. Ignoring her sister, she moved a quart jar of tomatoes to the proper shelf.

Maybe Ellie wouldn't come down the steps if she didn't think she was there. Maybe her sister would just go away and forget about her. Maybe her family and everyone in Honeycomb would forget she existed, and Willa could simply live there in the cellar. She eyed the wooden shelves her father had built for her *mam* in better days. There was certainly enough food down here to keep her alive for some time.

Willa knew it was a ridiculous notion, but she felt ridiculous today. And embarrassed by the mess she'd made of her life when she hired the matchmaker. Her *mam* had once told Willa that she was the most impulsive of her chicks and had warned her repeatedly of the danger of her actions. Her mother was right; Willa had been a child, then a teenager who made rash decisions. She thought she'd outgrown her reckless behavior but obviously, she hadn't. Otherwise, she wouldn't have gone to Sara's.

What had she been thinking? She'd been so upset and heartbroken that her and Aaron's feelings for each other had not been equal that having a matchmaker choose a husband for her had seemed logical. But it didn't feel that way anymore.

With the passing of time and seeing Aaron daily at the store, she was no longer angry. Now she was mostly sad. It had been a revelation to her that she still loved him. In the past, whenever she broke up with someone or he with her, the man was gone from her mind within days. She thought of Aaron every waking hour. It didn't matter that he had refused to marry her. Now she understood unrequited love and how painful it was.

With the final Christmas rush upon them, it was nearly impossible to avoid Aaron at the store, although she'd certainly tried, at least at first. Not only were folks buying cookies and take-out meals, but also holiday greenery and live trees from Elden and Millie's farm. And as much as Willa hated to admit it, it wasn't terrible working with Aaron. Things had been normal today as they conversed about various store-related topics.

It had gone so well that Willa thought maybe she had gotten over her disappointment. She even told herself that she was looking forward to meeting the man Sara would choose for her. But then, just before closing, Willa had seen Aaron talking with Maggie. The love in his eyes for his daughter, the smile on Maggie's face as she gazed up at her father, had erased any hope that she was recovering from her heartbreak. Aaron had caught her watching them and asked if he could speak to her privately. That was when she'd fallen apart. She'd told him no and barely made it out of the store before she'd burst into tears. And then she'd hidden in the farmhouse basement.

"Willa! Are you down there?" Eleanor called. "*Dat* thought you were, but then he said it might just be a mouse he heard open the basement door." Her sister raised her voice this time. "Willa!"

"I'm in the canning room," Willa called back. She listened to her sister's footsteps on the stairs and then on the concrete floor. Light filled the first room as Eleanor made her way to the second where Willa was working.

"What are you doing down here? You gave us a fright," Eleanor chastised as she entered the room, carrying a battery lantern. "Jane said you went out the back door and she saw you cutting across the field to go home. We looked everywhere for you. Supper's ready."

Willa spied a jar of beets with the green beans and moved it to its proper place. "These shelves are a mess. I thought I'd straighten them up."

"Tonight? After you worked twelve hours at the store?" Eleanor raised an eyebrow. "And you voluntarily came down here—" she glanced around "—with all the spiders?"

Eleanor was making a joke. Willa had a reputation for not liking icky things, but she couldn't bring herself to smile. Because she'd come to realize that she was miserable without Aaron and even more miserable now that she had hired the matchmaker.

When Willa came up with the idea, she'd told herself that if she couldn't marry the man she loved, at least she could marry a man she'd get along with. Not all marriages begin as love matches. She remembered her mother saying that days before her death. The decision had seemed perfectly logical a week ago. Willa trusted Sara Yoder more than she trusted herself to choose a husband, that was for sure.

Willa was more miserable now than when Aaron told her he wouldn't marry her. Against her will, her eyes filled with tears as she turned her back to her sister.

Eleanor exhaled heavily and set her lantern

down next to Willa's on a wobbly table in the basement. "Oh, Willa, I hate to see you like this."

She continued moving jars, using a damp cloth to wipe any that were dusty.

"I have a confession to make," Eleanor continued after Willa said nothing. "I think I made a mistake. *Nay...* I *know* I made one." Her voice was thick with emotion. "Seeing you like this. Seeing Aaron so lost... I believe I selfishly convinced myself that you and he couldn't marry." She hesitated and then continued. "But that's not true."

Willa continued with her task, trying to let her sister's words wash over her. Nothing Ellie could say or do now could change anything. Sara Yoder was choosing a husband for her. What was done was done. What would be would be.

"I told myself and I told you that you couldn't marry Aaron because you were Amish and he wasn't," Eleanor went on. "I convinced myself that what mattered to me was you leaving our church and the Amish Old Order. I was *so* sure of myself. But I realized this morning after prayer that that's not why I was so upset when I saw how you two looked at each other. Then when Judy saw you together. I didn't really care what people thought. I didn't believe that a decent man wouldn't marry you. That was a terrible thing to say. I wasn't worried about you leaving the church, Willa." Her voice caught in her throat.

Fresh tears ran down Willa's cheeks at the emotion in her sister's voice.

"I know now that I wasn't afraid of you leaving the church. I was afraid of you leaving Honeycomb. Leaving us. Leaving *me*," she murmured choking up. "Willa, please. Will you look at me?"

Wiping her tears, Willa slowly faced her but said nothing. There was nothing *to* say. She'd made up her mind when Aaron refused to marry her and now she was on a different path from which there was no turning back.

"I was wrong," Eleanor repeated. "You and Aaron can marry if you want to. You can now that he's found his faith again, found a church home. He told me he has plans to join the Mennonite Church again."

"Ellie," Willa said.

"*Nay*, hear me out, *schweschter*. The answer is clear to me now. I know that Aaron can't become Old Order again. He told me that weeks ago before I knew something was between you. But there's no reason why you couldn't become Mennonite. You haven't been baptized. Then you can live here in Honeycomb together, you and Aaron and Maggie." She hurried on. "Other young Amish folks have done it in Honeycomb and other communities in the county. I know you could do it. You'd fit easily into the life of a Mennonite woman *and* their church's beliefs, which aren't that different from ours."

A lump rose in Willa's throat as she stared at the concrete floor.

Eleanor moved closer. "You and Aaron could marry and…and stay here. But if you decided to leave Honeycomb, so be it. That's your choice. It's not mine. I want you here, but I want you to be happy more."

Willa slowly raised her gaze until she met her sister's. Eleanor also had tears in her eyes, and she tried to take her hand.

Willa didn't let her. "It doesn't matter," she heard herself say, her tone resolute. "None of it matters now. It's too late."

"What do you mean?" Ellie drew back. "I know you love Aaron and he loves—"

"I said it's too late, Eleanor," Willa interrupted, unable to hear another word. "Last week I went to see Sara Yoder. I hired her to find me a husband."

"You what?" Eleanor asked in shock.

"I hired the matchmaker, *schweschter*. I'll soon be betrothed."

Eleanor was silent for a moment, then shrugged. "So, tell her you changed your mind."

Willa shook her head. "*Nay.* No more impulsive behavior. I contracted with the matchmaker and the matter is closed. I'll marry who Sara says I should marry."

"Will you at least talk to Aaron about the possibility?" Eleanor begged. "He told me after you left today that he's been trying to broach the subject for days, but you wouldn't let him speak the minute you weren't talking about store matters. Just talk to him, Willa? For me, if not for yourself?"

"I will not. It's too late." Willa straightened her spine resolutely, even though she wanted desperately to say yes. It had never occurred to her that she could become a Mennonite. It was too late, she told herself.

"Stop being so stubborn. Don't lose your chance for love like this," Eleanor insisted. "Don't you see how happy our sisters are, all who married for love?"

"My mind is made up." Willa reached for her lantern. "Sara thinks she can have a husband picked out by Christmas Eve. I asked her to bring him to the luncheon. Now come on. Let's not make Jane and *Dat* wait on us for supper." She headed toward the outside entrance.

Eleanor took up her lantern and followed. "Willa, wait. You can't—you shouldn't do anything so rash. You—"

"I did what you wanted," Willa said, climbing the cellar steps into the dark, cold night. "This was your idea in the first place. Remember?"

"Yes, but that was because—"

Willa didn't let her go on. She couldn't bear to hear any more. "I've made my decision. I'll marry the man the matchmaker chooses for me. I don't want to hear another word on the matter. Not ever." She sounded so sure of herself as those last words tumbled out, but inside she felt like she was crumbling and soon there would be nothing left of the woman she had once known.

Aaron sat behind his desk in the store office and again hit the clear button on his desk calculator. He groaned and glanced at the black-and-white clock on the wall. The store didn't close for another twenty minutes, but he seriously considered quitting for the day. He could try again tomorrow to make sense of the numbers swimming on the paper in front of him. It wasn't like he'd be cutting out early. He was paid for forty hours of work, Monday through Saturday. Eleanor said from day one that he could choose his hours as long as he got his tasks done, and he'd probably already worked eighty hours in the last seven days. That morning, he'd left Maggie asleep in bed to come down at 5:00 a.m. After two cups of coffee and a cinnamon roll alone in the store kitchen, he'd stocked shelves out front and moved new inventory to the apartment. When Eleanor arrived at 6:30, he was filing paperwork that neither had found the time to get to all week.

Eleanor had fussed with him about him working too much but he'd argued that everyone there was working too much and soon they'd all get a well-deserved holiday. Once the doors were locked at 6:00 p.m. on December 22, everyone would have off until January. They had been working too many hours: Eleanor, her sisters, Annie and the Amish women employed there part-time for the Christmas season. Even Mark and his crew had worked long hours to complete the addition.

After all the Koffmans had done for him and Maggie, it only seemed fair that he should work as hard as they did. His justification was solid and he told that to everyone who would listen. What he didn't say was that he was working hard so he didn't have time to think about Willa. She was all he thought about. He lay in bed for hours at night, his brain churning. He thought about the mess he had made with their love, and the possibility of a life together. It seemed there was no chance he could make things right, especially when she refused to talk to him about anything except the store or Maggie. That meant he had to keep himself busy, otherwise his regrets would drag him down and he wouldn't be able to be the father Maggie deserved.

"There you are." Eleanor walked into the office. "Last place I looked, of course." She raised her hands in exaggeration. "We have to make this fast. Willa and Maggie are going to fetch the mail. A little bird told us that your church sent Maggie a Christmas card, her first ever, and Willa wanted to be sure she had a chance to retrieve it herself."

Aaron stared at Eleanor suspiciously. She sounded almost giddy, which was unlike her.

"No time to waste," she declared, and closed the door. "We have to talk."

He rolled back in his office chair. "What about?"

Eleanor opened her brown eyes wide. "What do you think?" She walked behind her desk and rolled her chair around to face his desk. "You and Willa, of course." She waggled her index finger, pointing to him and then toward the mailbox on the road.

He closed his eyes. "Nothing to talk about," he said quietly.

She sat in the chair and rolled it forward until her elbows were on his desk. "I disagree. We have a lot to talk about and not much time. We'll have to move on this if we're going to make it happen. Christmas Eve is a week from today, Aaron!"

He had no idea what she was talking about. Had he missed something she'd said? He was getting so little sleep that his brain hadn't been working properly; his struggle with paperwork proved that. He reached for his mug of coffee and took a swallow. It was cold and bitter… like he was likely to end up if he didn't snap out of this mood of his. He took another gulp. "You're going to have to back up, Ellie. I'm not following."

"*Nay*, we're not backing up." She slapped her hand on his desk, startling him. "We're moving forward quickly before my sister ruins her life and yours and Maggie's."

Who was this woman? he wondered. She looked like the astute, clever, strong-minded boss who had hired him, but this was a side of Eleanor Koffman he hadn't seen before.

"We're talking about Willa and you," she said impatiently. "We have to patch things up between you before she marries some chicken farmer from Kentucky. You know she hates chickens almost as much as spiders."

He shook his head rapidly. She had his brain completely rattled. "Willa's marrying *what* chicken farmer? Ellie, you're not making sense."

She took a deep breath and sat back. “I’m sorry. I’ve got dozens of things going on in my head.” She chuckled. “I suppose I do sound *narrish*. That means—”

“I know what it means,” he interrupted. “I spoke only Pennsylvania *Deitsch* until I went to school and learned English, remember? Same as you.”

“I did know that.” She clasped her hands on his desk as if in prayer and met his gaze. “So… back to Willa.” She cleared her throat. “If you don’t know this about her, you’ll learn it over time, but Willa can be rash. She can get a bee under her bonnet and make impulsive decisions that she regrets later. Now that she’s older, we don’t see it often, but I suspect that’s what’s happened here. It all started when she got angry at me. Then she told you she wanted to run away with you, and you said no.” She held up a finger. “Wisely. But that’s when Willa acted without thinking.”

Aaron was shocked that Eleanor knew what had happened. Did he not know Willa any better than he knew Ellie? “She told you she asked me to marry her?”

Eleanor made a face. “Of course not. Jane told me.”

He tilted his head, not quite believing it. He knew Willa and her sisters were close but he also knew Willa well enough to know that if she had any regrets about what she said or did that day, she wouldn't be eager to share it with anyone. "Willa told Jane?" he asked slowly. That didn't make any more sense than her telling her oldest sister.

Eleanor shook her head. "No. Jane was eavesdropping. She heard my conversation with Willa and then yours with Willa."

"And what exactly *was* your conversation with Willa?"

She sighed. "We don't have time to go over this whole thing. Hopefully, you and Willa will have the opportunity to do that later." She glanced down but then lifted her gaze to meet his. "My aunt saw you both outside in the dark at Henry and Chandler's place. I'm sorry, Aaron, but I told her she had to stop seeing you."

He nodded, starting to get the gist of what had happened the day Willa came tearing up the stairs, declaring her love for him and wanting to elope and run away. He didn't doubt that she loved him, not that day and not now. He had seen it before she spoke the words, but now he understood her urgency. Her impulsiveness, as Eleanor had suggested.

"And I was wrong to lash out at Willa that day. I know now that my reaction to my aunt's visit wasn't about you two as a couple, what people might say or even her remaining in our church."

Eleanor's words *even her remaining in our church* tickled at the edges of his thoughts as she continued talking. Where was she going with this? Did Ellie really think there was a way for him and Willa to be together as man and wife? She had his full attention now.

"It was more about me and what I wanted *for* me, Aaron. And I'm sorry for that. I hope you can forgive me."

"Of course I forgive you," he said, unsure for what. "But let's get back to Willa marrying a chicken farmer." He crossed his arms. "What did you mean?"

"Also my fault," Eleanor told him. "You see, just before you arrived that morning that you came into our lives, I suggested to Willa that she talk with a matchmaker. Sara Yoder. I'd been worried Willa wouldn't find a husband. I know you know she's dated a lot of men and nothing ever seemed to work out for her. I'd prayed that morning asking *Gott* to bring her a husband. And then I thought His answer was my idea of hiring a matchmaker for her." Her face softened. "I realize now that He did answer my prayers, answered all our prayers, when you and Maggie came to Honeycomb."

Her words touched his heart. He recognized that Eleanor had become like a sister to him. He didn't know how it happened or why… Had this been God's plan all along? He had prayed on his knees before leaving Paraguay with Maggie, asking God to guide them safely to a better life. Had it been the Koffmans he'd been meant to be near, not his blood relatives? Had God brought him to Willa?

But have I ruined everything by telling her I wouldn't marry her? He hung his head.

"Are you still listening to me?" Eleanor asked, impatience in her voice.

He made himself look at her.

"Willa hired the matchmaker without telling us. In…in her disappointment, desperation, I don't know." She waved her hand dismissively. "Out of heartbreak."

He wanted to hang his head again but didn't because if Eleanor thought he still might have a chance with Willa, maybe he did.

"Willa told the matchmaker that she would marry the man she picked out for her. Sight unseen, I suppose."

"She *what*?" he asked in disbelief.

"She said the matchmaker is bringing this man to the Christmas Eve luncheon. We have much to do, Aaron, if you want to marry my sister. If you want her to be a mother to Maggie. So do you?"

He blinked, overwhelmed. Hopeful. Afraid to be too hopeful. "If…do you think there's still a chance that—"

"Yes or no, Aaron. I have a plan. I'm not sure it will work, but it might. But I have to know, do you love her? Do you want to marry Willa if she's willing to convert and become Mennonite?"

"I do. Of course I do, but she was talking about a justice of the peace and moving to Arizona."

Eleanor chuckled. "That sounds like one of the ridiculous things she might say, but she would never marry any way but before *Gott*."

She smiled and that was when Aaron realized he did have a chance to hold Willa in his arms again. "Yes, I love Willa and I want to marry her, Ellie. Tell me what I need to do."

She glanced at the door. "I can't tell you all the details right now. She and Maggie will be back from the mailbox any minute. But you need to go to your church and speak to someone. Mark will know who. Find out what you need to do to marry in the Mennonite Church. What Willa needs to do. I'm going to speak to my uncle. I know he'll resist the idea of his niece marrying outside the church, but he's a good man and knows many of your church's congregants. It might take some convincing, but if our uncle can give his blessing, our community will. Maybe even our aunt."

This time they both smiled.

"Okay." He nodded. "I think Maggie is going to your place for supper and to help with something for the luncheon next week. If that's okay, I can track Mark down now and find out who we need to talk to."

"Good. Good." She nodded. "I'll see my uncle in the morning. We made cranberry streusel. I'll take some to him. He's always in a better mood with a plate of sweets in front of him."

"Okay. After we talk to those folks, then what?" Aaron asked. "Do you think Willa will sit down and listen to us? Will she talk to me? I've been trying for over a week and she won't give me a chance."

Eleanor exhaled. "I think part of the problem now that she's calmed down is that she knows she was hasty in hiring the matchmaker. But she's stubborn, especially when she knows she's made a mistake. I know my sister, and even though she loves you, she may feel like she has to go through with the match, even if she knows it's not right now. Sort of a 'You dug your grave, now lie in it' type of thing," she explained grimly.

"This all sounds good." He shook his head. "But how do I get Willa to agree to leave the Amish Church, join mine and marry me if she won't even speak to me?"

"Don't worry." Eleanor stood. "I have a plan."

"Papa! Papa!" Maggie called from somewhere in the store. "I got a Christmas card, Papa!"

"Here they come." Eleanor opened the office door and he heard the pounding of his daughter's boots on the hardwood.

"We'll talk tomorrow, Aaron."

He nodded, dazed, but the possibility that he might have a chance with Willa was exhilarating.

"And have faith," Eleanor insisted. "That if *Gott* meant you two to be together, you'll be man and wife, despite my sister's mistakes."

"Papa, look!" Maggie shook a card and its envelope as she burst into the room. "Look, Papa, I got a card with a baby on it. It's baby Jesus!"

Aaron pushed his chair back from his desk to make room for Maggie in her pink puffy coat to hurl herself into his arms. He took the card from her and looked over her head to see Eleanor in the doorway. "Thank you," he mouthed.

She smiled. "Thank me Christmas Eve when all has turned out as we pray it should."

Chapter Fourteen

Willa peered into the large mirror over their store's bathroom sink. Jane had recently installed it, claiming that because customers were permitted to use the restroom, it should be more conventional than a traditional Amish one. Willa had secretly suspected that was Jane's excuse to justify a mirror that allowed Jane to see herself from the waist up, but she appreciated it on a day like today.

Willa had dressed carefully in a new dark green dress that complemented her complexion and brown eyes. She'd chosen not to wear an apron because she wouldn't need it. Eleanor had told her that morning that she didn't want Willa to help serve the meal at the luncheon because she'd gotten word from the matchmaker that the guest they were all eager to meet would be there. Eleanor said that Willa should spend her time getting to know the young man instead of serving pineapple-glazed ham and egg casseroles to volunteers.

After her first reaction, Ellie hadn't protested Willa's decision to hire Sara to find her a husband any further. Maybe her big sister had finally recognized that Willa could make her own decisions. Or at least she accepted that Willa was resigned to marry the man the matchmaker chose for her. Either way, Willa was relieved that Eleanor wasn't angry with her. She wanted no bad feelings between them. She would need her sisters' support in the coming months as she moved on to the next stage in her life.

Willa leaned closer to the mirror and pinched her cheeks. She looked pale today, paler than usual for this time of year. Was she coming down with something or was this the look of a woman afraid to come out of the bathroom?

On her way to bed the previous night, Jane had pulled Willa aside and told her it wasn't too late to cancel the matchmaker. Her sister had offered to tell Sara in the morning, sparing Willa the embarrassment of changing her mind. When Willa said she wouldn't do that, Jane became angry. She accused Willa of acting rashly and stubbornly to the point that she was willing to make another bad choice to save face. Shorter than Willa, Jane had gotten in her face and told her this wasn't the way to do it even if she wanted the matchmaker to find her a husband. Jane said she might be inexperienced in matters of love but was certain that entering a marriage contract with one man while still in love with another was a recipe for disaster.

Willa had stoically thanked her sister for her unsolicited opinion and barely made it behind the closed door of her bedroom before she burst into tears. She knew that Jane was at least partly right. If she wanted to hire the matchmaker, why now? Why had she agreed to marry a man she had never met?

Another part of Willa believed that while she may have gone about this wrong, *Gott* wouldn't allow her to make a terrible mistake. If Sara brought a husband for Willa to the luncheon, didn't that mean he was the man *He* wanted her to marry? Everyone in the county said that Sara Yoder made the best matches. Surely that was by *Gott*'s hand, wasn't it? Why else would Sara have such an excellent reputation for so many years?

Once she'd settled down after her run-in with Jane, Willa had prayed for a long time. When she'd finally fallen asleep, exhausted, she had been at peace, convinced that *Gott* was with her. She still believed that this morning, though her hands were shaky and her stomach was topsy-turvy. That was only nerves, she told herself. Everyone who agreed to an arranged marriage was nervous, weren't they? The man she was about to marry was likely as nervous as she was. All she had to do now was find the courage to meet him.

A knock on the door startled Willa.

"Willa? Are you in there?" Eleanor called. "We could use a little help. Everyone is arriving at once. Early!" she explained, a nervous energy in her tone. Her sister loved organizing events but then fretted they wouldn't go well. They always did. "Why do they always come early?" she fussed.

Willa felt her heart racing in her chest. If folks were arriving, did that mean Sara was here? With her husband-to-be? She wanted to ask her sister but couldn't bring herself to do it. She was too anxious. Instead, she responded in what she hoped was a normal voice. She couldn't let anyone know she was having doubts. "*Ya.* Be right out." She glanced in the mirror again, smoothed her prayer *kapp* and marched to the door.

Eleanor was waiting for her in the hall. "I know I said you didn't have to work today."

She laid her hand on Willa's shoulder, which had an oddly calming effect. "You won't have to serve, not with you looking so pretty." She eyed her up and down. "You'll be too busy for that anyway." She pressed her lips together, stifling what looked to be a giggle.

Willa had never, in her life, heard her big sister giggle and she tilted her head to look at her suspiciously. Eleanor didn't have some plan to prevent her from meeting this man, did she? Was that why she had been behaving amicably the last few days? Or was Willa being paranoid? "What do you want me to do?"

"Plate the rest of the appetizers. We have stuffed eggs, pickles and olives, and sausage cheese balls. The sausage balls are already plated and being kept warm in the oven. As we discussed, the starters will go to each table to share. I was going to do it myself, but I ran out of time going back to the house for serving spoons."

The original plan had been to hold the luncheon at their home, their logic being that the event would feel more personal. However, when thirty-two people responded that they would be joining the large Koffman family, it had been decided that holding it at the store made more sense. It had been Aaron's idea. At first, Willa thought it would be too much work to move all the shelving out of the room to make space for tables, benches and chairs. It made sense, however, when he reminded them that they planned to move them anyway to clean and polish the wood floors during the Christmas break.

Willa glanced in the direction of the sales floor. She heard conversation and laughter and folks moving about. She hadn't detected Sara's distinctive voice yet, though. She returned her attention to her sister. "You only want me to plate? I don't have to bring the appetizers out?"

"*Nay.* Stay in the kitchen until Sara comes for you. That's her request."

Willa clutched her hands. "She's here?"

Eleanor nodded, pressing her lips together as if to prevent herself from saying something.

Again, Willa felt a creeping sense of wariness. "And…and the man?"

"*Ya*, a few men are here, too. We invited anyone who helped."

Willa couldn't tell if her sister was being serious or teasing. "I mean, is *he* here? The man Sara's chosen for me."

Eleanor broke into the most beautiful smile. "He is."

"And what do you think?" Willa asked, her heart rate picking up again.

"*Schweschter*, it doesn't matter what I think. I've accepted that you'll marry the man Sara thought best for you. Now it's nearly time to have brunch with him," she added gently.

Willa stared at the floor. Was she going to do this? She nodded with resolve. She *was* going to do it. She glanced up. "Is he handsome…or at least pleasing to the eye?" Her voice trembled.

Again, Ellie smiled. "He *is* handsome. Now

come on. Get those appetizers plated while I welcome our guests. I'll send Sara into the kitchen once she gets him settled."

As Eleanor walked away, Willa called after her. "Is he from around here or far away?" Suddenly she was afraid. Had she told Sara she didn't want to leave Honeycomb? "I don't want to move to another state, Ellie."

Her sister looked over her shoulder. "Stop worrying. You won't have to leave. Unless you want to, Willa. Now go on." She pointed to the kitchen. "Everything is going to be all right. You're going to be all right."

Willa let her sister go ahead of her and then walked down the hall, now curious about what local Sara had matched her with. Willa thought she knew every single man in the county. In the kitchen, she found Maggie standing on a step stool at the center island, transferring stuffed olives into a dish. She wore a red corduroy dress, black tights, little black boots and red ribbons in her braided hair.

For some reason, seeing the girl calmed Willa. "Look at you, getting things ready for the luncheon." She kissed the back of Maggie's head as she went by. She smelled of the soothing scents of fabric softener and baby shampoo. On the far side of the room, Willa took two large trays of deviled eggs from the refrigerator.

"I'm helping. Ellie said olives go in these dishes," Maggie said, pointing to the white bowls in front of her.

There were twelve cereal-size glass bowls on the island and one smaller one. There were also twelve egg plates with divots to seat deviled eggs nicely for display. But there was also a small one that only served four halves. Willa set the tray on the counter and washed her hands. When she returned, she studied the dishes. The twelve of each made sense. They had set up six dining tables so there would be two appetizer plates on each table. But what were the little plates for?

"Eggs go in these," Maggie told Willa, pointing at the stack of egg plates. She carefully lifted one olive from a jar with her spoon and rolled it into one of the bowls. "If you make a mess on the plate, you clean it with that," she instructed, nodding toward a damp dishrag on the counter. "Ellie said, and Papa says she's the boss."

Willa couldn't resist a sad smile; the simple reference to Aaron hurt. "I won't make a mess, but if I do, I'll be sure to tidy up," Willa agreed.

They worked in silence with Willa occasionally glancing at the girl. She hoped that once she was married, she would still be able to see

Maggie. She couldn't imagine her life without the little girl.

Or her father…

Willa picked up another egg plate. The stuffing had been piped into the egg halves and looked so pretty, especially with the pimento on top. "I suppose your papa is around somewhere?" she asked.

Maggie nodded as she continued to plate the olives.

"Doing things for Ellie?" Willa wasn't sure why she was torturing herself like this. The only way to get over Aaron was to stop thinking about it.

Maggie shook her head.

"No?"

"No," Maggie said, reaching for another bowl. "He's upstairs getting dressed. He has a new sweater and new shoes. He shaved, too." She stroked her cheek. "Now he's soft like me, he said." She wrinkled her nose. "But he's not."

Those little details made Willa smile again and she was trying to figure out how to get more out of Maggie when Jane, Cora and Annie bustled in.

"All done, I hope," Jane said, sounding as bossy as Eleanor. "We need to get these on the table!"

"Just about," Willa answered, wiping the edge

of an egg plate. She watched as her sisters and friend loaded trays to carry them out. "Eleanor said I'm to stay here and wait for Sara."

"*Ya*, you should wait here," Annie agreed, looking as if she might burst with excitement.

"Did you see him?" Willa asked, tugging at her friend's sleeve.

Annie nodded, grinning.

"And?" Willa asked. She was so anxious now that she wanted to run back to the cellar. But her days of acting impulsively were over.

Willa's sisters grinned but said nothing.

"Just have to wait and see!" Annie declared, heading toward the laughter and folks talking in English and Pennsylvania *Deitsch*.

Willa watched the women leave, one by one, with Maggie bringing up the rear, carrying a small tray with three small dishes.

Sara Yoder passed Maggie on her way into the kitchen. "Ready?" she asked, her face round and smiling. She looked almost as excited as Annie. Before Willa could respond, the matchmaker went on. "We didn't talk about this before because I didn't want to overwhelm you, but I have ground rules for couples meeting for the first time."

Willa gulped, straightening her posture.

"First impressions are important, but as I told you, you must control your initial response. The man I introduce you to may not be what you expect." The matchmaker held up a finger with authority. "But that doesn't mean he's not a good match."

Willa clasped her hands tightly, her heart pounding so hard that she feared it might come out of her chest. "I understand," she managed, wondering what he looked like. Ellie *said* he was handsome, but she knew that didn't matter. What mattered was what kind of man he was, what kind of husband and, *Gott* willing, father he would be. While an arranged marriage didn't start with love, she knew they could grow into it over time. She had to focus on that and not the love she had lost.

"Are you ready to meet the man who will be your husband?" Sara asked, her dark-eyed gaze meeting Willa's.

Willa was nearly frozen with fear. A voice in her head told her it wasn't too late to back out, but a stronger voice told her to trust in the Almighty. She nodded to Sara.

The matchmaker smiled, looping her arm through Willa's. "Let's meet your intended." As they walked down the short passageway between the kitchen and the showroom, the older woman whispered, "Don't look so frightened. I've made a good match on this one. One of my best, I promise you."

When they walked into the store's main room, it looked much bigger than usual with all the shelves and merchandise pushed to the back wall. At once, Willa was overwhelmed by the voices and confusion of fifty-odd family and friends settling into chairs and onto benches at long tables. Each was covered with a snowy-white tablecloth and decorated with white candles surrounded by pine boughs, red poinsettias and twigs of holly, heavy with red berries. There were white-china place settings with polished flatware. The familiar room seemed unfamiliar, smelling of cinnamon and evergreens and a blur of sights, sounds and smells. She saw her sisters, their husbands, friends from the community, and even Mark and Annie, but she identified no strangers.

Willa's forehead creased as she glanced at Sara, who was still holding on to her. "Where is he?" she whispered.

Smiling, Sara pointed.

In front of the bank of windows along the east wall, Willa saw a small table set for lunch for two. As with the larger tables, there was a white tablecloth, decorations and two place settings. She recognized the table that seemed out of place at once. It was the courting table she had seen in the matchmaker's kitchen. But the two chairs facing each other were empty. She started to ask Sara where her husband-to-be was when she saw the silhouette of a man. His back was to her, gazing out the window at the field dusted with snow. He wore slacks and a dark blue sweater, not Amish clothes.

She knew who it was before he turned.

Willa's breath caught in her throat. She wanted to run again but didn't know in which direction. Did she want to run away from Aaron or toward him?

The matchmaker gripped Willa's arm as if aware she might flee. "You asked me to make the best match I could and there he is."

"But, Sara—"

"Eleanor asked me to fix what she believed wasn't broken. Concessions will have to be made on both sides, but your bishops have already been contacted and the way paved for you both by those who care for you the most."

"I don't—" Willa couldn't speak. Her mind was flying in so many directions at once. This couldn't be possible, could it? Could Aaron love her enough to want to marry her?

"Your family was already in agreement that you and Aaron were meant to be husband and wife, and so was I once I interviewed him," the matchmaker said.

"But—"

"No *buts*," Sara chastised kindly. "Aaron

loves you and you love him, I'm told. And when there's love, Willa, particulars of where you'll live, how you'll make a living, even where you'll worship, become less significant."

Willa stared at Sara, afraid to look at Aaron. Her first instinct was to protest, argue and walk away, but she didn't want that. What she wanted was to love Aaron, to be loved by him. Forever.

"Go to him," the older woman said, releasing Willa. "Sit. Talk. See how you feel now about him. I won't hold you to the promise of wedding the man I choose for you today, but I'll be disappointed if you don't give this a chance. And so will that one."

In the direction Sara was pointing, Willa glanced over her shoulder to see Maggie on her knees on a bench between Eleanor and Jane. The little girl smiled, giving Willa the nerve to go to Aaron.

It seemed like a mile to the windows, though it was only a dozen steps. Thankfully, Aaron spoke first.

"I was afraid you were going to run when you saw it was me," he said almost bashfully.

"I was afraid I might," she admitted. When she gazed up at his handsome, clean-shaven face into his brown eyes, she felt her heart swell with love for him. Suddenly she was so thankful for her family, for Eleanor. Thankful they had prevented her from ruining her life with her rash and stubborn behavior.

"I'm glad you didn't run, Willa," he whispered. "Because if you had, I don't know what I would have done—" His voice caught in his throat and it took him a moment to recover and go on. "I know there's a lot for us to talk about and this isn't exactly the order of how things are supposed to go." He took her hand and suddenly it seemed as if only the two of them were in a room of fifty people. "But… Will you marry me, Willa?"

His hand was so warm and comforting that there was nothing she could say but what she knew in her heart were the only words she *could* say. "*Ya*, I'll marry you," she whispered.

He glanced toward the tables of guests who had suddenly gotten very quiet and then back at Willa. Holding her gaze, he slowly lifted her hand and kissed her curled fingers. "Thank you," he whispered. "You've made me a happy man, and that will be one happy little girl when we tell her our news."

Willa looked at Maggie, who waved at them. Willa waved back and then turned to him again. "Aaron, I'm so sorry for what I—"

"Not now," he interrupted. "There will be time to voice our regrets later. And our hopes and our dreams. Right now, though, I think we need to sit down."

"We do? Why?"

He nodded toward the others; his eyes danced with mischief. "Because while I'm sure everyone is pleased with our engagement, I think they want to eat."

They laughed together and Aaron led her to the table for two. They sat down and clasped their hands together as Ellie encouraged everyone to say a silent grace. Instead of closing her eyes in prayer as usual, Willa gazed at her husband-to-be across the table and thanked God for him, for Maggie, and for all the days of joy she knew were to come.

Epilogue

Five Years Later
Grand Canyon, Arizona

Willa took Aaron's hand as she stepped down from the shuttle bus and inhaled Arizona's hot, dry air. "Are we here finally?" she asked, slinging her small backpack over her shoulder.

"We're here." Aaron grinned. "And we go this way." Hand in hand, they wove through the crowd of tourists, following the paved path and the signs indicating which way to go. "First stop, Hopi Point."

Willa was so excited that she didn't know which way to look. The desert was so different from the lush green of Delaware that she'd felt like she was on a different planet since they landed in Phoenix. There was so much to see, and the food was amazing. The tacos, rice, and beans were nothing like what they made at home, but they were so delicious that she wanted to buy a cookbook for Ellie before they left. With authentic recipes, they might be able to add some Mexican-style entrées to their restaurant menu.

"I wish Maggie could have come with us. She would love this," Willa said, studying the stunted plants that grew in the arid soil.

"She would," Aaron agreed. "And maybe we'll make this a family trip once the children are a bit older, but this adventure is just for us, right? A belated honeymoon."

Walking beside her husband, she gazed into his brown eyes. She couldn't stop smiling. When she and Aaron had married four years ago, she knew she had made the right decision. Ultimately, when she stood in the Mennonite church and wed him, there was nothing reckless about it. As they exchanged their vows, she knew that Aaron was the man *Gott* had always intended for her. Every day she woke to her smiling husband and every night she said a prayer thanking *Gott* for the gift of Aaron and Maggie and their growing family.

"Here we are, Hopi Point." Aaron led her to an iron rail.

Willa took in the panoramic view of the canyon below, looking east to west. She was overwhelmed by the beauty of the towering cliffs and colorful rock layers. The skirt of her dress whipped in the hot wind, flapping at her legs. She dressed as she always had for the summer in a modest dress and sneakers. However, she no longer wore her hair twisted at the nape of her neck with a *kapp* over it, and her dress had a small floral pattern, something that she would never have done as a member of the Old Order Amish.

"My puzzle doesn't do it justice, does it?" she asked, leaning on the metal rail and looking up at her husband.

He smiled and tucked a lock of her blond hair that had escaped her ponytail behind her ear. It was windy there on the lookout. "I don't know. I can't get a good look because my wife's beauty outshines anything, even a view from the rim of the Grand Canyon."

She laughed, giving him a playful push, and then moved closer to him. "Thank you for this," she said. "I've dreamt of seeing this since I was a little girl."

"You're welcome. I'm only sorry it took us so long to get here." He smiled mischievously at her.

She lifted her shoulder and let it fall. "Two sets of twins in four years, we've had our hands full. Especially with you and Ellie adding a restaurant to the store." She pushed the hair out of her eyes, gazing at his handsome face. "I'm just glad Ruthie and Emma were old enough to finally be left at home." Her brow furrowed when she thought about how much she missed her children. "It was okay to leave them, *ya*?"

"Of course. Ellie and Beth are taking good care of them, I promise." He slipped his arm around her waist and they stood side by side looking down on the Colorado River that wove its way through the canyon. "All five children are fine. We talked to Maggie this morning. She's having a great time with her *endies* and says her brothers and sisters are as happy as they can be." He kissed her temple. "Let's enjoy this time alone together, shall we?"

Willa gazed into her husband's eyes and surprised him by kissing him on the lips, right there at the rim of the Grand Canyon for anyone to see. They didn't usually kiss in public, but this was a special occasion, if there ever was one.

He drew back, grinning. "Why'd you do that?"

She shrugged, smiling up at him, knowing that as much as she loved her husband today, she would love him more tomorrow. "Because I can."

* * * * *

Dear Reader,

I'm so pleased you could join me in the Amish community of Honeycomb again. It's such a joy to see old friends and make new ones, isn't it? I'm relieved that Willa has finally found the man who was meant to be her husband. She and Aaron are so perfect for each other!

Now, with this story complete, I'm thinking about what comes next. Eleanor is determined to never marry, but sometimes God's plan for us differs from our own. I think she will also have a husband and children with time. The question is, who has God chosen for her, and will she listen? After all, she does have a stubborn streak, just like Willa. Be sure to look for Eleanor's story in the spring of 2025.

Until we meet again, may you be blessed.
Emma Miller